Oh, Lord, he was in love. How had that happened?

How could a man suddenly find he was deeply in love with a woman and not have been aware of his changing feelings?

Love sure was sneaky, Ted decided. Powerful, potent...and sneaky.

His first reaction was shock. That shifted almost instantly to pure joy. An incredible warmth suffused him, and he had the urge to shout his declaration from the rooftops.

But then...

Then it really began sinking in. And it felt like a punch in the gut.

He, confirmed bachelor Theodore Sharpe, was in love with pretty, *pregnant* Hannah Johnson.

Ah, damn. What a mess!

* * *

"Robin Elliott sheds her pseudonym to write under her own name—the popular and beloved Joan Elliott Pickart."
—Harriet Klausner, *Affaire de Coeur*

Dear Reader,

Spring is just beginning in the month of April for Special Edition!

Award-winning author Laurie Paige presents our THAT'S MY BABY! title for the month, *Molly Darling*. Take one ranching single dad, a proper schoolteacher and an irresistible baby girl, and romance is sure to follow. Don't miss this wonderful story that is sure to melt your heart!

Passions are running high when *New York Times* bestselling author Nora Roberts pits a charming ladies' man against his match—this MacKade brother just doesn't know what hit him in *The Fall of Shane MacKade*, the fourth book in Nora's series, THE MACKADE BROTHERS. Trisha Alexander's new series of weddings and babies, THREE BRIDES AND A BABY, begins this month with *A Bride for Luke*. And Joan Elliott Pickart's THE BABY BET series continues in April with *The Father of Her Child*. Rounding out the month is Jennifer Mikels with the tender *Expecting: Baby*, and Judith Yates's warm family tale, *A Will and a Wedding*.

A whole season of love and romance has just begun from Special Edition! I hope you enjoy each and every story to come!

Sincerely,

Tara Gavin
Senior Editor

Please address questions and book requests to:
Silhouette Reader Service
U.S.: 3010 Walden Ave., P.O. Box 1325, Buffalo, NY 14269
Canadian: P.O. Box 609, Fort Erie, Ont. L2A 5X3

JOAN
ELLIOTT PICKART

THE FATHER OF HER CHILD

Silhouette®

SPECIAL EDITION®

Published by Silhouette Books
America's Publisher of Contemporary Romance

For Ryan Schmidt,
my friend

 SILHOUETTE BOOKS

ISBN 0-373-24025-2

THE FATHER OF HER CHILD

Printed in U.S.A.

JOAN ELLIOTT PICKART

is the author of over sixty-five novels. When she isn't writing, she enjoys watching football, knitting, reading, gardening and attending craft shows on the town square. Joan has three daughters and a fantastic little grandson. Her three dogs and one cat allow her to live with them in a cozy cottage in a charming small town in the high pine country of Arizona.

Chapter One

Ted Sharpe leaned against the wall of the elevator, closed his eyes and drew a weary breath.

He could easily fall asleep standing right here on his feet, he thought. He'd just ride the elevator up and down for ten or twelve hours until he had rejuvenated his tired body.

If anyone poked him and questioned what he was doing there, he'd switch into his tough-cop mode and tell them he was on official elevator-security detail. That ought to impress 'em.

He and his partner, Ryan MacAllister, had pulled a double shift of duty in their patrol car, due to the fact that the Labor Day weekend brought people flocking to Ventura and the surrounding area. It was the last hurrah of summer, and the party goers did it up royally, overindulging in food, drink and reckless driving.

Police officers all along the California coast were kept busy, hauling in the drunken drivers and the brawlers who lost their common sense for the duration of the extra-long holiday weekend.

But now, midmorning on Tuesday, things were back to normal, as though someone had waved a magic wand and restored peace and order. People had returned to work, some a bit worse for wear, the visitors had exited and Ventura was once again as it should be.

Sleep, Ted thought foggily as the elevator bumped to a gentle stop at his floor. His kingdom for a long stretch of blissful, uninterrupted sleep.

The doors swished open and he left the elevator. His feet felt as though they weighed a hundred pounds each. As he plodded along the carpeted hallway, he absently noted that the door to the apartment before his was ajar and two men in white coveralls were coming out, leaving the door open behind them.

The men stopped in their tracks when they saw Ted, a common reaction when suddenly confronting a police officer in full uniform.

In spite of his bone-deep fatigue, Ted cataloged a detailed description of the pair, including the red stitching above the pockets on the upper left of the front of their uniforms. The red thread spelled out the message that they represented Ace Moving and Storage, one of them was Pete, the other was Jake.

"Hi," Pete said. "Nice day, huh?"

Ted stopped his sluggish trek. "Yep. You must be moving someone in. The previous tenant left a couple of weeks ago."

"You live in this building?" Jake said.

Ted nodded. "Next apartment."

"Good," Pete said, smiling for the first time. "We've had the cops called on us twice in the past year. People watch television one night, see a dumb flick about robberies pulled off by guys posing as moving men, and the next day...bingo...they're reaching for the phone when we show up at the house next door. What a hassle."

Ted smiled and nodded. "My partner and I went out on a call like that a few years ago. It was a false alarm, just like you're talking about. You guys are covered today. That place has been empty, so there's nothing to rip off. You have to be bringing stuff in, not out."

"Are we ever," Pete said. "The big pieces don't fit in the elevator. We just hauled a sofa up four very long flights of stairs. We're really earning our pay on this one."

"Well, enjoy," Ted said, starting away. "Me? I'm hitting the cool sheets. Someone could probably rip off the whole building, brick by brick, and I'd sleep right through it."

"See ya," Jake said.

"Yep," Ted mumbled.

As he entered his apartment, he gave fleeting thought to the fact that he should have asked ole Pete and Jake about the person, or persons, who were moving in. His previous neighbor had been a mousy little guy, an accountant, who was as quiet as the mouse he looked like.

Since Ted had the last apartment on the floor, he only had one close neighbor to be concerned about, as far as noise sifting through the connecting wall. A tiny, elderly widow lived directly above him on the fifth floor, and he never heard her footsteps.

A man on shift work was very often asleep while others were awake, and neighbors could play a bigger role than normal in his life.

Yeah, he thought, removing his gun and holster. He definitely should have asked the movers about who was taking up residence beyond the mutual wall. Well, too bad. He was so beat, he didn't have the energy to retrace his steps. He'd just wait and be surprised. Pleasantly surprised, he hoped. Yep, he was casting his vote for another mousy accountant.

Ted yawned three times in succession as he stripped off his clothes, then sighed in pleasure as he sank onto the unmade bed, pulling the rumpled sheet and blankets over his naked body.

"Mmm," he said at the sheer ecstasy of the soft pillow cushioning his head.

Within moments, he was asleep, wrapped in a protective cocoon of soothing silence.

Two hours later, Ted shot straight up in bed, his heart beating wildly. He'd been having a rather nondescript, boring dream. He'd been ambling through a huge grocery store, pushing a cart and tossing things in without bothering to see what he was taking from the shelves. The dream no doubt meant that he was hungry.

So what had jolted him awake?

A sound reached him and he shook his head in disbelief, attempting to dispel the lingering fogginess of sleep.

He was now, he knew, wide awake, and the noise was real, not a leftover memory from the dream. He was hearing . . . Yes, it was a piano being played with a great deal of enthusiasm *and* volume. Someone was pounding out "Yankee Doodle" on a piano!

"No way," Ted said, flinging back the blankets. He left the bed and pulled on the uniform trousers that he had dumped on the floor in a heap. "Not a chance. I need sleep. I'm going to *get* some sleep. Mr. Doodle can take a hike."

Adding nothing more to his limited apparel, he strode from the bedroom with heavy, angry steps. Leaving the apartment, he stopped for a moment to determine the source of the music.

"Mmm," he said, starting down the hallway.

The door to the apartment next to his was open, as it had been earlier. Ted went to the doorway, intent on marching right in and making it clear to the merry music-maker that playing the piano at an ear-splitting level was not remotely close to acceptable. Not when the closest neighbor was a wiped-out cop who had just gotten off a grueling double shift.

Instead, he took one step into the living room and stopped so suddenly that he teetered for a second. His eyes widened, and he had to order himself to close his mouth that had dropped open as he took in the view before him.

The piano was on the far side of the room at an odd angle, as though not yet placed in its designated spot by the movers. The piano player was facing him, although obviously unaware he was there.

The "Yankee Doodle" enthusiast was a woman.

And she was absolutely beautiful.

Because several cartons were stacked next to the piano, Ted could only see the woman's face and shoulders.

Like a cameo, he thought. Lovely.

She had silky black hair that swung in graceful waves around her face and brushed the tops of her shoulders as she moved her head to the beat of the peppy tune. Her eyes were large and very dark, further accentuating her fair skin. Her features were delicate...femininity personified.

And she was smiling.

Man, oh, man, Ted thought as heat rocketed through his body. This woman could wake him up any day of the week if she wanted to. He would wholeheartedly prefer, however, that when she did, she be next to him in bed, wearing nothing more than that pretty smile.

Forget the mousy accountant type. This was a new neighbor a man could *really* appreciate.

No, now wait a minute, he thought in the next instant. His rapidly heating-up body was running roughshod over his mind. Gorgeous or not, the lady had to be made to understand that pounding on a piano was not socially correct apartment-living behavior.

Ted moved farther into the room, stopped, crossed his arms over his bare chest and cleared his throat to gain the woman's attention.

She continued her rousing rendition of "Yankee Doodle."

"Hey," he yelled, "Ms. Doodle. Could I have a minute of your time here?"

Hannah Johnson jerked at the sudden bellowing sound of a man's voice, her hands crashing onto the piano keys. She snapped her head up, then stared at the man standing in the middle of her cluttered living room.

Heavenly days, she thought. *From where had this half-naked, magnificent specimen of a man come?* He was tall, with blond, sun-streaked tousled hair, tanned skin and the bluest eyes she'd ever seen.

His shoulders were wide, his chest broad, his arms nicely muscled. The curly hair on his chest was a shade darker than the hair on his head. His features were rugged, removing him from the pretty-boy arena to a place clearly labeled *male.*

Oh, yes, he was gorgeous.

But if the volume of his voice and the frown on his face were clues to his frame of mind, he was not a happy camper. So, what was Mr. Body Beautiful's problem?

"Hello," she said pleasantly. "You startled me. I'm Hannah Johnson."

"Ted Sharpe," he said gruffly. "I'm your neighbor." He nodded briskly in the direction of his apartment. "I live next door. I also *sleep* over there when I'm not jarred awake by a piano concert."

"Oh, I see," Hannah said slowly. "You're a late sleeper? It *is* past noon, you know."

"I realize that, but I've only been asleep for two hours. Ms. Doodle, I'm a cop. I just put in a helluva double shift. I need sleep. Are you with me here? *Knock off pounding on that damn piano.*"

Hannah matched his frown. "There's no call to be rude, Mr. Sharpe. A quiet explanation as to the fact that I was disturbing you would have sufficed." She slid her eyes over him from head to toe. "Do you always greet your neighbors half-naked?"

"I'm half-dressed. You're lucky I stopped long enough to put on my pants before I came over here. A dead-tired man who is blasted out of a sound sleep by a lousy rendition of 'Yankee Doodle' is not in a friendly-neighbor mind-set."

"Lousy rendition? Lousy! I'll have you know, Mr. Sharpe, that I play the piano extremely well. Thank you very much."

"No, you play very *loud.*"

"You really are rude. What happened to the motto of 'Policemen are our friends'?"

"It got blown away by 'Yankee Doodle.' I assume we've reached an understanding here? If you're going to play that damn thing, *do it quietly.*"

"Or what? You'll arrest me?"

Ted nodded. "You've got it, darlin'. I'll slap you with a citation for disturbing the peace, Ms. Doodle."

"Johnson. It's Hannah Johnson."

"Whatever."

"And I'll have *you* arrested for indecent exposure. You can't waltz into my home half-naked."

"Like I said, I'm half-dressed. And your door was open. You don't have a case."

"My door," she said, "is about to be closed. Behind you. After you leave. Now." She got to her feet and came around the stack of cartons.

Ted's eyes widened as he stared at her.

Ms. Doodle, his mind hammered, *was pregnant!*

"You're pregnant," he said.

"Really? Gosh, I'm glad you pointed that out. I wondered what this funny lump was under my blouse. My, my, I'm going to have a baby. I certainly appreciate your telling me that, Mr. Sharpe."

Ted rolled his eyes heavenward. "You must drive your husband totally nuts. You've got a real temper there, Mrs. Doodle."

"It's *Ms.* Doodle. I mean, *Ms.* Johnson. I'm divorced, Mr. Sharpe. There's no husband to drive totally nuts. I sincerely hope for the sake of Mrs. Sharpe that there *isn't* a Mrs. Sharpe. You are *not* a pleasant man."

"There's no Mrs. Sharpe, and I can be as pleasant as the next guy, once I've had a decent stretch of sleep."

"Fine," she said, starting toward him. "Go tuck yourself back in bed with your teddy bear. If I decide to play the piano, I'll do it more quietly."

"Thank you," Ted said, glaring at her.

Just then, Pete and Jake entered the room carrying boxes, which they set on the floor.

"That's the last of it," Pete said. He took a clip-board from the top of one of the cartons. "If you'll sign this receipt, we'll be on our way." He glanced at Ted. "Let me guess. You got yourself mugged and they ripped off your cop suit."

"Cute," Ted said.

Hannah signed the paper, thanked the men, then followed them to the door.

Pregnant, Ted thought, watching her. *Divorced and pregnant.* Ms. Doodle had a lot to deal with on her own. She sure was feisty, though; gave as good as she got.

Did she have a family who would be showing up to help her unpack, move furniture, set this mess to rights? Hell, what difference did it make? It was re-ally none of his business.

After Pete and Jake disappeared, Hannah stood with one hand on the doorknob.

"Good day, Mr. Sharpe," she said, lifting her chin.

Ted dragged one hand through his already sleep-tousled hair, then started slowly forward, finally stopping in front of Hannah. He looked directly into her eyes, realizing they were so dark he could hardly discern the pupils.

"Look," he said, "I apologize for storming in here and yelling my head off. Exhaustion is no excuse for being...um..."

"Rude," Hannah supplied.

"Yeah, okay, I was rude, and I'm sorry."

Hannah sighed. "Well, I'm not without fault, Mr. Sharpe. I was feeling a bit overwhelmed by this move, the mess, the general confusion of it all. I've found that by playing an upbeat tune on the piano, I can often gather myself together.

"I've been living in a house, and I now realize that apartment dwelling is going to require some changes in my behavior. I'm sorry that I woke you."

"Let's start over, shall we?" Ted extended his hand. "Hello, Ms. Doodle, I'm Ted Sharpe, your neighbor. Would you like to borrow a cup of sugar?"

Hannah smiled, then tentatively raised her hand to place it in Ted's.

"Hello, Ted," she said, her smile fading. "Thank you for the offer, but I have sugar somewhere in this disaster area."

Dear heaven, she thought, Ted Sharpe was even better looking up close than from across the room. She'd never seen such blue eyes, and they were framed by long, blond lashes. He had tiny lines by those incredible eyes, created from squinting against the California sun, or maybe from smiling that knock-'em-dead smile of his.

His hand was big and warm, so very warm, and the heat was traveling up her arm and across her breasts. That chest . . . so broad, tanned and beautifully muscled. The hair there caused her fingertips to tingle with the urge to touch, then weave, through the enticing curls.

Oh, Hannah, she admonished herself. *What on earth is the matter with you? Retrieve your hand. Right now!*

She started to remove her hand from Ted's, only to have him tighten his hold enough to keep it firmly in his.

The beautiful Ms. Doodle, he thought. *Hannah.* It was an old-fashioned name and it suited her perfectly. She really was as lovely as a cameo picture, with her dark, dark eyes and hair, and her skin that would feel, he just somehow knew, like ivory velvet when he caressed it.

When? his mind echoed. *Whoa, Sharpe, hold it right there.* The last thing Ted needed in his life was to get involved with a woman who was going to have a baby in a few months. He kept his social scene uncomplicated; easy come, easy go. And he only dated women who played the game by those rules.

Yes, Hannah Johnson was enchanting.

No, he wasn't going to do more than say hello to her if they happened to pass each other in the hall.

"May I have my hand back now, please?" Hannah said quietly.

"Your what?" Ted blinked. "Oh, your hand." He released it quickly, as though it had suddenly become a hot potato. He glanced around the cluttered room. "When I moved into this building, I had the movers put my furniture in place. Your buddies Pete and Jake shouldn't have left things like this."

"That was our agreement. They gave me two estimates for the move. I took the less expensive one, which means they brought in my belongings and plunked them down."

"Is your family coming over to help you get squared away?"

"I have no family, Mr. . . . Ted, but several of my friends will be here after school to pitch in."

"School?"

"Summer vacation is over and classes started today, but I'm on leave for this school year. I taught music appreciation at an elementary school."

Ted nodded. "I see. I bet those little kids could really belt out 'Yankee Doodle.'"

"They certainly could," she said, laughing.

Oh, hell, Ted thought, that cooked it. Hannah's laughter was like tinkling bells. A coiling heat steadily built low in his body. He had to get out of here and safely back to his own bed.

"Well, it sounds like you're all set," he said, "so I'll go catch some more z's. It was nice meeting you, Ms. Doodle, once we got past the war."

Hannah raised her right hand. "I solemnly swear I won't play the piano for the remainder of the afternoon."

"My tired body will certainly appreciate that. I'll see ya."

Ted left the apartment, strode down the hall to his own and hurried inside.

Hannah stood in her doorway until Ted disappeared, then continued to stand there, staring at the empty hallway.

A swift kick from the baby caused her to jerk in surprise, come out of her somewhat hazy state and step back into the living room. She closed the door, turned to survey the clutter, then allowed herself to execute a long, weary sigh.

"Well, Ms. Doodle," she said aloud, "unpack a box, or two, or three. Oh, ugh."

She started across the room, but changed her direction and went to the piano, gently lowering the cover

over the keys. She shifted her gaze to the wall separating her apartment from Ted's.

"Sleep well, Officer Sharpe," she said, saluting the wall.

Smiling, she took the lid off the nearest box.

Late that night, Hannah turned off the small lamp on the nightstand next to her bed, then shifted into a more comfortable position beneath the blankets. As she closed her eyes with a weary sigh, her hands floated upward to rest on her stomach.

"Good night, little one," she whispered.

As though hearing the softly spoken words, the baby moved, then stilled.

So tired, Hannah thought. Oh, goodness, she was exhausted. Even with the help of four friends from school, getting the apartment into a livable condition had been very hard work. There were still boxes to unpack, but she'd run out of energy and had finally quit for the day.

Her friends had been wonderful, pitching in like troopers and moving the furniture into place. One of the women had discovered the box of linens, then had made up Hannah's bed, stating it would be ready and waiting for Hannah to climb into.

They'd sent out for pizza for dinner, insisting that Hannah take a break and put her feet up. The two men had toted the emptied packing boxes down to the Dumpster, and except for a half-dozen small cartons, her home was in order.

Home.

This was it. This medium-size, two-bedroom apartment was now her home. Oh, how quickly her life had changed, falling apart and shattering hopes and dreams for the future, as well as the trust and belief in the man she'd vowed to love until death parted them.

A man she'd never really known at all.

A man who turned out to be far, far different than who he presented himself to be when they had married over two years ago.

"Go to sleep, Hannah," she told herself.

She'd get an energy-restoring night's sleep and wake up in the morning refreshed in mind and body. Wake up in her new home.

While Hannah's friends had been there, everything had been dandy. They were busy working, laughing, talking. The teachers had shared the tales of woe of the first day back at school.

But finally they'd gone, each hugging her, saying they'd see her soon, that they would keep in constant touch.

And then it had been so quiet.

Exhaustion had swept over Hannah like a heavy cloak, accompanied by the silence that seemed to have an oppressive weight of its own.

She'd taken the lid off a box, stared at the contents as though she'd never seen them before in her life, then thrown up her hands in defeat.

After a warm bath, she'd gone to bed, the soft pillow feeling heavenly as she lowered her head onto it. It was *her* familiar pillow, *her* bed, *her* sheets and blankets.

But how long would it be until this place really felt like *her* home?

"Attitude, Hannah," she said to the darkness. "It's all in the attitude."

The apartment was cheery, with sunny rooms that were spacious enough to hold the furniture she'd kept. The piano was polished and ready for her to give private lessons to her young students.

She'd shop tomorrow for more food for the cupboards, unpack the last of the boxes, and everything would be shipshape.

She could start to make plans for the baby's nursery that would occupy the now-empty second bedroom. That would be fun, exciting.

Heavens, she even had a gorgeous hunk of man as a neighbor. She could gawk at him if she happened to see him in the elevator or hallway.

Ted Sharpe, she mused, smiling. How many women had a half-naked, drop-dead handsome man show up in their living room the day they moved into their new apartment? No, no, half-*dressed,* to quote Officer Sharpe.

And that was another thing to be grateful for. She had a policeman living right next door in case a band of thieves tried to break in. How lucky could a woman alone get?

A woman alone.

Oh, dear, Hannah thought, she mustn't dwell on *that* while she was so tired. She'd frighten herself to death if she gave further thought to going through the remainder of her pregnancy, the birth of the baby, then raising the child, all alone.

Facts were facts. She *was* alone. She was twenty-five years old, divorced, pregnant and alone. So be it. She and this baby she loved and wanted with every breath in her body would be *all right*. Whatever came along, she would handle it, one day at a time.

Two tears slid down Hannah's cheeks and she dashed them away angrily. She was overtired, that was all. Overtired and momentarily overwhelmed by everything. She was going to sleep. Right now.

"I'm trying, Gran," she whispered with a wobbly little sob. "I'll be fine tomorrow. Yes, in the morning there will be daffodils and daisies."

Chapter Two

Ted and his partner, Ryan, had the next two days off, then they would go on a three-week duty shift of straight days, meaning their working hours would match those of an average businessman.

While Ryan MacAllister eagerly anticipated the rotation of duty that brought him straight days so he could spend more time with his family, Ted Sharpe saw it as a ticket to the busy social life he enjoyed.

The two men led lives that were at opposite ends of the poles, yet had been close friends for many years. The endless hours they spent together cruising the streets of Ventura in their patrol car had resulted in many intimate conversations on topics they wouldn't consider sharing with anyone else.

There was also the special bond between them formed from the knowledge that each would risk his life for the other if the need arose in the line of duty. Their friendship, therefore, went even deeper than most brothers'.

When Ted left his apartment in the early morning, he glanced at Hannah Johnson's door as he passed it, idly wondering if her teacher friends had shown up as promised to give her a hand straightening out the mess in her apartment.

Ms. Doodle had been good on her word. No further piano playing had disturbed Ted's sleep the previous day, and he'd awakened refreshed.

As he rode down in the elevator, Ted frowned.

Hannah must have been in a helluva rotten marriage, he thought, to get divorced while pregnant, then have to move and settle into a new place. He assumed she had divorced her husband, rather than the man divorcing her.

Either way, Ted decided, the guy must be a real scum to have the situation end up for Hannah as it had. She was young, didn't look more than twenty-four or twenty-five, and had said she had no family. *That was rough, really rough.*

Ted dropped his laundry off at the establishment he always used, knowing it would be ready for him to pick up the next day.

Ryan had razzed him unmercifully about being too lazy to wash his own socks and underwear. But Ted's one attempt at tackling the chore had resulted in an entire wash emerging a strange shade of puce.

After taking his uniforms to the cleaners used by many of the police officers, Ted headed for Ryan's house. Today, they were scheduled to put the last touches on the redwood deck they'd built onto the back of the MacAllister home.

During the drive to Ryan's, Ted's mind floated once again to Hannah Johnson. Did any of her teacher friends include her in their family celebrations? he wondered. Where did she spend Thanksgiving and Christmas? On her birthday, did someone bake her a cake?

An even bigger question, Ted thought dryly, was why he was using his mental energies thinking about such stuff? *Maybe it was because he was on his way to Ryan's.*

The MacAllisters were a large family of warm, loving people, who considered Ted one of the clan. He, himself, was an only child, and his parents lived in a retirement community in Arizona. He managed to see them several times a year, and they had a good time whenever they got together.

His mother was a gem. His father? Well, they did all right during short visits, but that special bond with his dad had been broken ever since...

Ted automatically jerked his thoughts from the direction they were headed. He wouldn't allow his mind to travel down that road.

He was thinking about... *Yes, okay, Ms. Doodle.* She was a safe subject, as it might be weeks before he even saw her again, in the hallway or elevator.

Did Hannah have a family, Ted's thoughts continued, the way he did with the MacAllisters? Were there people who would take on the roles of aunts and uncles for her baby? Were there kids for her child to play with, grow up with?

Ted chuckled. There was *definitely* a slew of kids bouncing around at the MacAllister gatherings.

Michael, the oldest son, and his wife, Jenny, had a son, Bobby. Forrest MacAllister and his wife, Jillian, had triplet girls. *Triplets.* The adorable little girls had celebrated their first birthday a couple of weeks ago. *Man, were they cute. And busy!*

Ryan's sister, Andrea MacAllister, was married to John Stewart, and their twins, Noel and Matt, were always bundles of energy. And Ted's partner, Ryan, and his wife, Deedee, had a son they'd named after Ted. Theodore Ryan MacAllister, called Teddy, would be a year old around Thanksgiving.

Ted would never forget how proud, how touched he'd been, when Deedee and Ryan had announced they were naming their son after him. They had been convinced they were expecting a girl.

But Forrest, The Baby Bet champion of the family, had declared that all pink rabbit toys would have to go on a shelf because Deedee was going to have a boy.

And Forrest had never lost The Baby Bet.

How did he do it? It was getting creepy, the way Forrest always won.

Yeah, those MacAllisters were something special, including Margaret and Robert, the parents of the group. Did Hannah have a family like that who made her feel as though she belonged? Ted wondered.

Hell, he didn't know. And since Ryan's house was just up ahead, he didn't have to think about it any longer, nor wonder why he was dwelling on the subject at all.

Ryan and Deedee MacAllister lived in a modest, three-bedroom ranch style home on a standard, subdivision-size lot. Robert MacAllister and sons Michael and Forrest, as well as daughter, Andrea, were architects, all of whom would have been delighted to design a made-to-order house for Ryan and Deedee.

Ryan, however, had been adamant about their living on a policeman's salary. Deedee had agreed, and the income from her store, Books and Books, was being invested for Teddy's college education, as well as their emergency-only fund.

Ted parked in the driveway, cut across the lawn to the front door and rang the bell. Deedee answered the summons with a smile.

"Hi, Ted," she said. "Come in."

He entered the house and immediately inhaled the delicious aroma of cinnamon.

"Mmm," he said. "Coffee cake?"

"Your favorite kind. I just took it out of the oven." Deedee laughed. "You're wiggling your nose like a pink rabbit."

"Hey, I'm a blue rabbit," Ted said, following her across the living room. "Do you suppose there's a contest we can enter Forrest in where we'd all make a bundle?"

"That's a thought," she said. "He's never lost The Baby Bet. I can remember when Michael said Forrest should be 'unchampioned,' but it hasn't happened. Forrest is incredible."

"Yep."

The pair entered the sunny kitchen to find Ryan just about to slip Teddy into his high chair.

"Whoa," Ted said. "We have a tradition, you know. Teddy has to be an airplane before he has coffee cake. Right, sport? We always do our airplane bit."

"'Pane," the baby said, holding out his arms toward Ted.

Ted took the baby from Ryan and held him high in the air while making roaring-engine noises. Teddy laughed in delight.

Ryan smiled at them, then poured coffee into three mugs decorated with brightly colored butterflies. Ryan MacAllister was tall, nicely built, very good-looking and a dedicated police officer.

When his first wife, Sherry, had been killed by a berserk gunman in the emergency room of the hospital where she worked, Ryan had quit the force and withdrawn from life for nearly two years.

His love for Deedee had brought him out of his near solitude to once again embrace each new day. He'd rejoined the police force as Ted's partner.

"Zoom," Ted said. "Ready to come in for a landing." He settled Teddy in the high chair. The baby began to pound happily on the plastic tray. "I turned off your engine, sport. What do you need? Fuel? Me, too. It's coffee cake time."

The coffee cake was served and Ted and Ryan discussed the final work to be done on the deck.

"The deck is going to be great," Deedee said. "We can sit out there, barbecue, watch Teddy tear around the yard. Thank you again, Ted, for helping Ryan build it.''

"That's about the fiftieth thank-you," Ted said. "Hey, I enjoyed it. It sure was different making something that size after working on my miniatures."

"I can imagine," Deedee said. "What kind of miniature are you carving now?"

"A tiny baby cradle, complete with rungs. It's tough, but very challenging. When I'm finished with it, the thing is supposed to rock back and forth like the tiny rocking chair I made. The rungs are a killer."

"I'd go nuts handling something that small," Ryan said. "You've said it's very relaxing, but I'd be a blithering idiot."

"Short trip, MacAllister," Ted said. "Great coffee cake, Deedee. Are you going into Books and Books today?"

"No, I'll work tomorrow while Teddy plays with Noel and Matt. Then I'll have the twins the next day so Andrea can put in some hours at MacAllister Architects. The triplets have the sniffles, so Jillian isn't in the baby-sitting trade-off routine this week."

"Three little kids with runny noses," Ted said, shaking his head. "They're probably cranky. What a handful they must be. For Ms. Doodle's sake, I hope she has one, only one, laid-back, easygoing type."

"Who?" Ryan said, placing another slice of coffee cake on his plate.

"Ms. Doodle?" Deedee said. "You've met a mother-to-be whose last name is Doodle?"

Ted chuckled. "No, her name is Johnson. Hannah Johnson. She moved into the apartment next to mine yesterday. I was dead tired and she woke me up playing 'Yankee Doodle' on the piano.''

"Uh-oh," Ryan said. "I can picture it clearly in my mind. You did *not* ask her politely and quietly to please lower the volume of the serenade."

"No-o-o, I didn't, and I was informed that I was extremely rude. Oh, and she hoped for the sake of Mrs. Sharpe that there *wasn't* a Mrs. Sharpe, because I was *not* a pleasant man."

Deedee laughed. "Good for Ms. Doodle. Ms. Is she married?"

"Divorced," Ted said. "She's a music teacher on leave and has teacher friends, but no family."

"Oh, dear, that's grim," Deedee said. "Divorced, no family and pregnant. That's a lot to handle. When is her baby due?"

Ted shrugged. "I don't know. She looks like she's hiding a volleyball under her shirt. How many months pregnant is a volleyball?"

"Oh, Lord," Ryan said. "Even *I* know every woman does this number differently. Deedee got to about beachball size with Teddy. Jillian was more like a life raft with the triplets."

"Amazing," Deedee said, shaking her head.

"What is?" Ryan said.

"That you've managed to stay alive as long as you have without being murdered, Ryan. Those are not flattering descriptions you're dishing out there, mister. Ted, is Hannah nice? Is she pretty?"

"Very nice, very pretty. Yeah, she's lovely."

Ted averted his eyes from Deedee's, and cut another slice of coffee cake. He lifted it onto his plate, then stared at it.

"Hannah reminds me of a cameo," he went on quietly. "She has dark hair and eyes, and very fair skin, like fine, porcelain china. Put that together with her old-fashioned name and...well, she's like a cameo." He cleared his throat. "Whatever. It's not important."

Deedee and Ryan exchanged quick glances, Ryan raising his eyebrows slightly as he looked at his wife.

"Uh-oh," Teddy said merrily. "Uh-oh, uh-oh."

"Out of the mouths of babes," Ryan said, grinning.

"What?" Ted said, looking over at him.

"Nothing, buddy. Finish stuffing your face, then we'll get to work."

"Okay."

"You're welcome to stay for dinner tonight, Ted," Deedee said. "We're going to officially christen the deck by Ryan barbecuing some steaks. I should have invited you sooner, but with the long hours you guys put in over the holiday, I wasn't certain you'd be doing the deck today."

"I appreciate the invitation," Ted said, "but I . . ."

"Have a date," Deedee said, laughing. "I swear, Ted Sharpe, your little black book must be bulging at the seams. Is there an unattached woman in Ventura and beyond that you *haven't* taken out?"

Ms. Doodle, Ted thought, then instantly frowned in self-disgust. Where had *that* come from? He had no intention of seeing Hannah Johnson socially. No way.

"There are a few left," he said, smiling. He popped the last bite of coffee cake into his mouth, then drained his mug. "MacAllister, let's do it. That deck is calling our names."

"Uh-oh," Teddy said again, then flung a handful of cake crumbs onto the floor.

"That settles it," Deedee said. "We've got to get a dog, Ryan. I need a furry vacuum cleaner to stand ready by Teddy's high chair."

"Good thought," Ryan said, getting to his feet. "We'll decide what kind of dog we want, then go to the pound or pet store."

"Let me know when you're going," Ted said, "and I'll tag along. I want to have a voice in the choice of my godson's first dog. It's a momentous event."

"It is?" Deedee said. "Well, okay, if you say so, Uncle Ted."

"I say so," he said firmly.

Late that afternoon, Ted parked in his numbered slot at the apartment complex, got out of his Blazer and locked it. As he started toward the building, he heard a car door slam and automatically turned in the direction of the sound.

Hannah was farther down the row of cars, juggling her purse and two large grocery sacks as she made her way slowly to the front of her car.

"Hey," Ted yelled, sprinting toward her. "Hold it right there."

Hannah stopped in surprise as Ted halted directly in front of her. In the next instant, he'd wrapped his arms around the sacks and snatched them from her grasp.

"What—"

"These are heavy," he said, shifting them against his chest. "You shouldn't be carrying stuff like this." He frowned. "Haven't you read books about dos and don'ts, the rules about being pregnant, what you can and can't do?"

"Of course I have," she said, matching his frown. "Those sacks aren't too heavy for me. The biggest problem was trying to see my feet while I was carrying them."

"Well, you watch your feet. I'll tote the groceries." He started away. "Come on."

Hannah hurried after him. "I can't decide if you're being rude again, or if I should thank you for the help."

Ted chuckled and a funny flutter whispered down Hannah's spine. She slid a glare at him from beneath her lashes.

"When is your baby due?" Ted asked, as they walked along the sidewalk.

"January first."

"A New Year's baby, huh? Well, that settles that mystery. A volleyball means five months' pregnant."

Hannah looked at her stomach, then back at Ted.

"A volleyball?" she said. "I'm as big as a volleyball?"

Ted nodded. "Yep. I was telling my partner, Ryan MacAllister, and his wife, Deedee, about you. You know, the fact that I had a new neighbor who is going to have a baby. Deedee wondered when your baby was due, and I said I hadn't asked, but your stomach looked like a volleyball."

"You were discussing my stomach with strangers?" Hannah said, her voice rising.

"No," he said, an expression of pure innocence on his face, "not strangers. They're like family to me. I'm the godfather of their son, who was named after me."

"You know what I meant."

"It just came up in conversation, that's all. Say, if you need any pregnant advice or whatever, there are a whole slew of MacAllisters who can answer your questions. They're good people, all of them. Not only that, they do babies one at a time, twins, even triplets. Jillian had three pretty little girls all in one pop."

"Goodness, what an overwhelming thought," Hannah said. She paused. "Jillian? Triplet girls? That rings a bell. I remember seeing an article in the paper a year or so ago about a well-known author giving birth to triplets. Jillian Jones-Jenkins. Yes, that's who it was. I've read several of her books. She's an excellent writer."

"That's Jillian. She's married to Forrest Mac-Allister, my partner's older brother. The triplets were a year old a couple of weeks ago. They're walking now. You should see them. They each pick a different direction and take off. They're not into the buddy system of traveling together."

Hannah laughed as she opened the door to the building, then stepped back to allow Ted to enter.

There was that tinkling-bell laughter, Ted thought, moving past her. And there was his body, going nuts again, with instant heat rocketing through him. Hannah looked so pretty. She was wearing dark slacks and a pink top that made her sort of . . . glow. *Yeah, glow.*

"You certainly seem fond of babies," Hannah said, bringing Ted from his thoughts.

They crossed the lobby and arrived at the elevators. Hannah pressed the button.

"Babies?" he said. "Yeah, I like the little critters. They're fascinating. It amazes me the way they have opinions, likes and dislikes, from the moment they're born. They're people in small packages."

Hannah laughed again and Ted nearly groaned aloud as the heat within him coiled tighter and lower.

"That's an interesting way to put it," she said. "But I guess you're right."

"Noel and Matt are Andrea and John's twins. Andrea is my partner's sister. From day one, Matt made it clear he wanted to sleep on his back. Noel yelled her head off if she wasn't put in the crib on her stomach. How in the heck do newborn babies know how they like to sleep?" Ted shook his head. "Amazing."

The doors to the elevator swished open and they entered, Hannah pushing the button for the fourth floor.

"Yes, you're definitely right," she said. "Babies are people who know their own minds from the moment they're born. I apparently haven't gotten to that chapter in the book yet." She sighed. "I have so much to learn before my baby is born."

"You'll be a great mother, Ms. Doodle. Your natural maternal instincts will kick in, you'll see. You'll be able to tell what the problem is from the way the munchkin cries. You know...hungry, wet, mad as hell. Trust me here. It's true."

"You're quite an expert, Officer Sharpe. You sound like a man who would thoroughly enjoy being a father."

"Me? No, no, I'll pass on that one. I'm a Professional Uncle. That's my official title, in capital letters."

"Ah, I see," she said, nodding. "I understand."

No, she didn't, Ted thought. No one knew the truth, not even his best friend, Ryan. And no one ever would.

At Hannah's apartment, she unlocked the door, pushed it open, then turned to face Ted.

"I'll take those sacks now," she said. "Thank you for carrying them up for me."

"I'll put them on your kitchen counter. Lead the way, ma'am."

They entered the living room and Hannah closed the door. Ted stopped and swept his gaze over the room.

"Very nice," he said. "You really shaped up this place. No one would know that you moved in just yesterday."

"My friends were marvelous," she said, starting toward the kitchen. "I only have a few small cartons left to unpack."

Ted followed her and set the groceries on the counter.

"Your furniture matches," he said, smiling. "Mine are leftovers from when my folks sold their house and retired to a smaller place in Arizona. I have one of these, one of those." He shrugged. "It suits me fine. I must admit, though, your place is very homey."

Hannah looked up at him quickly. "Homey? Like a home?"

"Yes."

"Oh. Well, that's good, very good. I—" She stopped speaking and shook her head. "Never mind." She took a can of peas out of one of the bags.

Ted removed the can from her hand, placed it on the counter, then gripping her shoulders gently, he turned her to face him.

"What were you going to say, Hannah? You suddenly sounded sort of . . . I don't know . . . sad."

"No, no, I . . ."

"Hannah," he said quietly. "Talk to me."

She took a step backward, forcing him to drop his hands to his sides.

"I just have a lot of adjustments to make, that's all," she said. "Things happened very quickly and at times it seems that I was swept along, totally out of control. Now I'm here, in this apartment, and it doesn't feel like it's mine yet, my home. Does that make sense?"

Ted nodded. "Sure." He paused. "Do you know what you need? A kitten."

"A kitten? What for?"

"To finish making this your home. You've got four months before the baby arrives. In the meantime, you need company, a kitten to greet you when you come in the door. You'll feed it, take care of it, talk to it, share your home with it."

"Well, maybe a kitten *would* make a difference. You know, add a sense of permanence to this place." She paused and frowned. "No, forget it. I could probably find a kitten in the For Free section of the newspaper, but I'd have to buy a litter box, food, that sandy stuff that goes in the box, take the kitten in for shots, all kinds of things. My budget is very tight and I have so much to get to be ready for the baby.''

"Okay, try this. I'll ask around the department, see if anyone has kitten equipment stashed in their garage. People get pets, something doesn't work out for whatever reason, and they have doghouses, cat boxes, all kinds of jazz just taking up storage space.''

"Well..."

"No harm in asking. Right?"

"Yes, all right. I'd appreciate that, Ted. Thank you. I seem to spend a lot of time thanking you for things.''

"I'm just being neighborly.''

"You're a very nice man, Ted Sharpe," she said softly.

Their eyes met. Dark, dark eyes looked deeply into eyes as blue as a summer sky. Heartbeats quickened and time lost meaning.

An invisible thread seemed to wrap itself around them, making it impossible to move or breathe. Heat thrummed in their bodies, and desire began to change the color of their eyes to smoky hues.

Hannah forced herself to tear her gaze from Ted's.

"I..." She drew a steadying breath, then turned toward the counter. "I'd better put away these groceries.''

Ted blinked, bringing himself back from a hazy, sensual place.

"Hannah, I..." He stopped speaking as he heard the rasp of passion in his voice.

"Thank you again, Ted," Hannah said, not looking at him as she took items from the bag. "Would you mind seeing yourself out? There's ice cream in here somewhere and it's probably getting soupy."

Ted stared at her for a long moment. "I'll be seeing you, Hannah," he said finally, then moved past her.

"Goodbye, Ted."

He hesitated, then kept going without looking at her again.

As she heard the door shut behind him, Hannah closed her eyes and gripped the edge of the counter.

Dear heaven, she thought. *What had come over her?*

Hannah opened her eyes again and continued unpacking the groceries with jerky motions.

She'd felt it, the heated pulse of desire deep within her as she'd been held immobile by Ted's mesmerizing blue eyes.

She was a pregnant woman, for mercy's sake, and she'd been consumed by desire for a man she hardly knew. That was disgusting, wanton, tacky. It probably wasn't even normal!

Well, she was putting the entire incident out of her mind.

And from now on, she was going to avoid any contact with Ted Sharpe. As far as she was concerned, the man did *not* exist.

Ted entered his apartment, slouched onto the sofa, then was on his feet again in the next instant. He began to pace the floor with heavy strides.

Get a grip, Sharpe, he ordered himself. *Calm down.* So, okay, he'd had a sexual reaction to Hannah. No problem. He was a healthy man, for crying out loud.

But Hannah was pregnant!

He'd wanted her, damn it, and the woman was pregnant. Was that sick? Shabby to the max? Hell, he didn't know.

What he *was* certain of was that from this very moment, he was going to cut a wide berth between himself and Ms. Doodle.

He was steering clear of Hannah Johnson!

Chapter Three

Ted did not see Hannah for the remainder of the week. He thought he heard the quiet playing of the piano on one occasion, but by the time he moved close to the wall connecting Hannah's apartment with his, there was no sound of music.

His Wednesday-night date was so-so at best. He took an advertising executive to dinner, but she spent the evening expounding on the various ad campaigns she was working on. She related every minute detail of the wording, the colors used, the length of time and where the ads would run and the psychological impact the ads would have on consumers.

While one of her dissertations would have been interesting, by the sixth one Ted was bored stiff and eager to take the chatty lady home.

His Friday-night date canceled due to a cold and he realized he was relieved that his evening was free. He simply wasn't in the mood to do the town. He'd dated the woman many times and knew she would expect him to spend the night in her bed. The fact that he wasn't in the mood for *that*, either, led him to wonder if he was on the brink of a mid-life crisis.

On Saturday morning, Ted was restless and edgy. He wandered around his apartment, rejected the idea of working on the miniature cradle, then vacuumed for lack of anything better to do, ignoring the fact that the cleaning service had been there the day before.

When the telephone rang shortly after lunch, Ted snatched the receiver, more than ready to hear the voice of another human being.

"Hello?" he said.

"Were you sitting on the phone? It didn't even do one full ring."

"Just happened to be standing right here, Ryan. What's doing?"

"There's a deal going on in the mall on Kennedy. The Friends of Animals are setting up in the parking lot with all kinds of pets they need to find homes for."

"Oh, yeah?"

"You make a donation, and you can also pay for a certificate for shots from a local vet. He's giving a portion of the fees to the organization. It's a good outfit. They take care of abandoned animals, and some people bring them litters of puppies and kittens that they can't deal with...stuff like that."

"I take it you're going over there to look for Teddy's dog?"

"Yes."

"I'll meet you there. What time?"

"Half an hour."

"Roger," Ted said, then replaced the receiver. He got to his feet. "Thank you, Officer MacAllister. I'm outta here."

A roped-off area of the mall parking lot was crowded with people walking down rows of boarded pens, wire carrying cases, bird cages and sundry other methods of containing a wide variety of animals.

Ted managed to find Ryan, Deedee and Teddy in the throng.

"Busy place," Ted said.

"That's for sure," Ryan said. "Well, let's browse. Teddy isn't going to be happy in that stroller for too long. He gets tired of looking at people's kneecaps."

"I don't blame him," Ted said. "What kind of dog are you thinking of getting?"

"Something medium-size," Deedee said. "Big enough to hold its own with Teddy, but not so enormous it will knock him over just by wagging its tail. I think it should be fairly young, not set in its ways. Teddy and the dog can grow up together."

"Sounds like a plan," Ted said. "Let's check it out."

They walked slowly down the first row, Teddy chattering happily in his stroller.

"Hey, there we go," Ryan said, smiling. "Rabbits. Want a rabbit, Ted?"

"I won't say in front of my godson what *y*ou can do with a rabbit, MacAllister. A dog, we want a *dog*."

Ryan whooped with laughter.

Twenty minutes later, Deedee stopped in front of a wire cage.

"Oh, look at that darling," she said.

"A beagle," Ryan said. He leaned forward to read the card attached to the cage. "Female. Six months old. Good with children. Housebroken. Owners moved out of state. Shots up-to-date."

Ted hunkered down and looked at the dog. The beagle wiggled and whined, her tail wagging with excitement.

"Would you like to hold her?" a woman said. "I'll open the cage, but don't let her run off. She's a busy girl. Her name is Scooter, but she's young enough to learn to answer to another name if you prefer."

"Yes, please open the cage," Deedee said. "She's so cute."

The woman unlatched the door and the dog bounded out. She whizzed passed Ted and went directly to the stroller. Planting her front paws on the stroller tray, she gave Teddy a sloppy kiss on the nose. The baby laughed in delight.

"Sold," Ted said, getting to his feet.

"I'd say so," Ryan said, chuckling. "We have instant rapport here. Deedee?"

"She's perfect, and I think the name Scooter is very appropriate."

The transaction was completed and the next stop was at a table selling collars and leashes. Scooter literally bounced along, causing Teddy to laugh and clap his tiny hands. A bag of food and two dishes were purchased.

"Would you like to come back to the house, Ted?" Deedee said. "We've got to take some pictures of Ms. Scooter MacAllister."

"No, thanks," Ted said. "I...um...I have some shopping to do." He ruffled Teddy's hair. "Enjoy your first dog, sport. She's a beauty."

Farewells were exchanged and Ted watched as the MacAllister quartet disappeared from view. Once they were out of sight, he spun around and made a beeline for the third row of pets.

Hannah massaged her aching lower back, then sat down on the sofa. She'd given four hours of private piano lessons to four wiggly young students that day, and her back was killing her.

She'd had a sandwich and a bowl of soup as an early dinner and now had to decide how she wished to spend the evening. During the past few months, she'd spent every spare moment sorting through household items, then packing what she wished to move to her new home.

Home, her mind echoed as she swept her gaze over the room. No, she wasn't going to dwell on that theme again tonight. In time, the apartment *would* seem like home. It was just a matter of adjustment and attitude, she kept telling herself.

With a decisive nod, she rested her hands on her stomach, smiled as she felt the baby move beneath her palms, then sighed.

What should she do with the long hours of the evening that loomed before her? Read a book? Work on the bib she was embroidering for the baby? Watch television? Go to the video store and rent a movie? No, she didn't have the energy for that. Forget renting a movie.

"Oh, I know," she said aloud.

She'd reread one of the novels she owned written by Jillian Jones-Jenkins. It would be fun because she sort of knew Jillian now. Well, that was stretching it a tad. She knew Ted, who knew Jillian.

Heavens, Jillian had given birth to triplet girls. She had three babies to tend to all at the same time. What an overwhelming and exhausting thought. Of course, Jillian no doubt could afford to hire help; a nanny, cleaning lady, maybe even a housekeeper who lived in and did the cooking as well as cleaning.

"I'll see my child now," Hannah said, poking her nose in the air. "Do be certain his nappy is dry. I can't abide a wet diaper." She fluttered one hand in the air to dismiss the obedient servant.

Laughing softly at her own silliness, Hannah shook her head, then stared into space.

Ted had said the triplets were very pretty, she mused, and were walking all over the place, each in a different direction. Ted certainly seemed fond of all the MacAllister babies. For a bachelor, he was amazingly involved in the little ones' lives.

What had he said his official title was? Oh, yes, he was a Professional Uncle. In capital letters, if you please. Strange. If he liked children so much, why didn't he get married and have a family of his own?

Hannah thought Ted appeared to be in his early thirties. Surely the swinging singles' life had lost some of its appeal by now. She'd hated that whole scene—

not that she'd taken a very active part in it. Ted must still like it, though, or he would have opted out. He was so gorgeous, Hannah was sure he could have his pick of the multitude of available women out there on the loose.

Ted Sharpe. Why on earth was she wasting her mental energy and time sitting here like a lump thinking about Officer Sharpe?

Just then, a knock sounded at the door. Hannah was grateful for the intrusion, realizing she wouldn't have to answer the question she'd just asked herself.

She went to the door and peered through the peephole.

"Ted," she whispered, her eyes widening.

Dear heaven, she'd made him materialize by thinking about him!

Oh, Hannah, stop it, she admonished herself, undoing the safety chain. What a ridiculous thought.

She opened the door.

"Hi," Ted said, smiling. "Here." He pushed a cardboard box at her. It had handles at the top and a series of holes along the sides.

"What," Hannah started to say, taking the box.

Ted lifted a large bag from the floor and moved past her into the living room.

"May I come in?" he said. "Thanks. I'm in." He turned and closed the door, snapping the lock into place. "I hope you weren't busy."

"No, I wasn't, but—"

"Good. Okay, let's unpack this stuff."

"Wait a minute," she said. "Oh," she gasped in the next instant, as a funny noise came from the box. "What's in this thing?"

Ted beamed at her. "Your kitten."

"My what?" She looked at the box, at Ted, then back at the box. "I don't have a kitten."

"Sure you do. It's in the box. Consider it a house-warming present. See, Teddy is really into throwing food on the floor when he's in his high chair. So, Deedee said they should get a dog to vacuum up the debris."

"Oh, well," Hannah said dryly, "that explains everything."

"Let me finish. I told Deedee and Ryan that a little kid getting his first dog is an important event, and as Teddy's godfather I should be there when they picked it out.

"An organization had a deal going today in the parking lot of a mall and we went over there. Teddy has a beagle puppy named Scooter. Cute dog. Teddy loves it. Anyway, they had all kinds of pets...even rabbits...so I got you a kitten."

"But..."

"Don't worry about a thing." Ted placed the sack on the sofa and began to pull things out. "You're all set. Here's a litter tray, a big box of litter, a scoop, a bunch of food and a ball with a bell inside.

"Oh, and this certificate entitles you to the shots the kitten needs. You go to the vet whose name and address is on here. Okay?"

"I can't allow you to buy me all of this, Ted."

"I already did," he said with a shrug. "When I was growing up, my mom baked a cake whenever new neighbors moved onto the block. She told me it was a way to say welcome. Believe me, Ms. Doodle, you would *not* want me to bake you a cake. So, I substituted a kitten instead."

"But—"

"Just say, 'Thanks, Ted.'"

Hannah smiled. "Thank you, Ted. Thank you so much. I shouldn't accept such a generous gift, but I'm going to. Oh, this is wonderful."

"Open the box."

Hannah set the carrying carton on the sofa and unlatched the cardboard handles. As she pulled the sides free, a furry, sandy-colored head popped up.

"Oh, how sweet," she said, picking up the kitten. She held the tiny bundle to her cheek. "It's so soft, so small."

"She's six weeks old. She. It's a girl. Cute, huh? I like her feet. All four feet are white, like she's wearing socks. Great tail, too. It's as long as her body. What are you going to name her?"

"Thank you."

Ted frowned. "Weird name."

"No, no, I just feel as though I should say thank you a hundred times," she said, smiling. She cuddled the kitten beneath her chin.

"Your eyes are sparkling," Ted said quietly. "I wouldn't have thought that eyes as dark as yours could sparkle, but they really are. You look...I don't know, Hannah...happy. Yeah, you look happy, and that's nice, really great."

"I . . ." Hannah stopped speaking as she shook her head, her eyes filling with tears. "Oh, dear, ignore me. I'm a classic case of a pregnant woman who cries at the slightest provocation.

"It's just that I can't remember when anyone has done such a thoughtful thing for me. Not since my gran." Two tears slid down her cheeks. "Oh, drat."

Ted smiled at her warmly, then framed her face in his hands and wiped the tears away with his thumbs in a soft, gentle motion.

A flutter of heat whispered along Hannah's spine.

"If you get weepy over a tiny little kitten," Ted said, "I'd hate to see what would happen if someone gave you a big horse. You'd probably flood the place."

Hannah managed to produce a trembling smile, but in the next instant it faded as she continued to look directly into the blue depths of Ted's eyes. His hands cradling her face stilled, but remained in place as he met her gaze.

A cameo, his mind hummed. So lovely. There Hannah stood, tears glistening in her incredible eyes, a tiny kitten tucked beneath her chin. She looked so young, vulnerable, so beautiful.

He wanted to wrap her up in a cocoon, protect her, take care of her, assure her that she wasn't alone. She had so much to deal with, so much to face, but *she wasn't alone* because *he* was there.

Sharpe, he ordered himself, *get a grip.*

Abruptly, he dropped his hands from her face and cleared his throat.

"So, Ms. Doodle," he said, looking at the paraphernalia spread out on the sofa, "let's get set up here. Where do you want the litter box?"

Damn it, he fumed, the heat low in his body was taking its sweet time to cool down. He ached for Hannah Johnson. He wanted her, wanted to make slow, gentle love to her for hours. What in the hell was this woman doing to him?

No, now wait. Ted cautioned himself. He was overreacting, panicking for no reason. She pushed his sexual buttons, but that was understandable because she was a lovely, desirable woman. The fact that she was volleyball-size pregnant didn't seem to enter into his sensual attraction to her, and it certainly didn't diminish it in any way.

As for his never-before-experienced emotions of protectiveness, of momentarily seeing himself as the one who would ease her burdens...well, that was understandable, too.

He was a cop who cared, a compassionate man who spent his life in the role of the knight to the rescue. He shielded the good from the bad, took care of those who couldn't fend for themselves.

Therefore, he mentally rambled on, it stood to reason that Hannah's plight would touch a chord, cause his police officer, protector-of-the-people instincts to rise to the fore.

Yes, sir, he had it all figured out.

There wasn't a thing to worry about in regard to his reactions to Hannah Johnson.

"What do you think?" Hannah said.

"What?" he said. "I'm sorry, I was daydreaming for a minute there."

"I said, I thought I'd put the litter box in the corner of the bathroom so it will be on a tile floor. That will be easier to clean if she tracks any of the litter."

Ted nodded. "Good plan." He picked up the tray and box. "Let's do it now, in case Her Highness gets a call of nature."

They tended to the litter box, then Hannah put a plastic place mat on the floor in the kitchen next to the refrigerator. She filled one bowl with food, another with water and put the kitten in front of it. She then offered Ted a soft drink.

"Sure," he said. "Thanks."

They settled onto opposite ends of the sofa with their drinks. The kitten finished eating, wandered back into the living room and crawled up on the sofa. She looked at Hannah, then climbed onto Ted's thigh, curled into a ball and went to sleep.

Hannah laughed. "Well, she definitely prefers men over women."

"She's missing a bet. I'm certain that your leg is much softer than mine and would make a nicer pillow." He ran one fingertip over the sleeping kitten's head. "Cute. I like her. She does need a name, though, Hannah."

"Daisy. I'm going to call her Daisy."

Ted nodded. "That works for me. It's very...girly."

"Well, it means more than that to me. It's a symbolic name."

Ted shifted his gaze from Daisy to Hannah. "Oh?"

"You see," she started, then hesitated, giving Ted the impression she was deciding whether or not to continue to say what had prompted her to name the kitten Daisy.

"I'm listening, Hannah."

"Yes, you are, aren't you?" She cocked her head slightly to one side as she studied him for a long moment. "You really are."

She was so fragile, Ted thought. She moved so tentatively, as though afraid the next step she took might hurt her in some way. Man, the guy she'd been married to must have been a scum from the word go.

"Well, you see," Hannah said, "I was raised by my grandmother, my gran, from the time I was three. My parents were killed in an automobile accident. My gran was a wonderful, warm, loving and wise person. I loved her very, very much."

"Loved? Past tense?"

"She died when I was twenty. I still miss her, and I think of her every day. When I was growing up, she'd tell me that whenever I had a bad day, a gloomy day, with problems or troubles of any kind, I should remember that tomorrow would be sunny and would bring me daffodils and daisies."

"Nice," Ted said. "Very nice."

"I can't begin to tell you how many times I've reached for that. Something upsetting would happen and I'd tell myself, 'Tomorrow will be sunny. I'll have daffodils and daisies.' It sounds silly, I suppose, but it has gotten me through some rough moments."

"Daffodils and daisies," Ted repeated, nodding.

"The kitten was such a wonderful surprise, such a thoughtful gift. She *is* going to help me feel this is my home now. She deserves the name Daisy, the way my gran taught it to me."

"I think I would have liked your gran."

"And she would have liked you, Ted."

Once again, time stopped as they looked into each other's eyes. Once again, the maddening heat coiled tight and low in Ted's body. Once again, Hannah felt the strange flutter dance along her spine.

Enough, Ted thought. Damn it, enough was enough.

He tore his gaze from Hannah's, then lifted the kitten from his thigh with both hands and set her gently on the sofa next to him. He got to his feet.

"I'd better shove off," he said, starting toward the door.

Hannah pushed herself from the soft cushion and followed him.

"Thank you again, Ted." She stood on tiptoe and kissed him on the cheek.

"Sure," he said, then hurried out the door.

Hannah locked it behind him, slid the safety chain into place and returned to the sofa. She cradled the sleeping kitten in both hands and lifted her to eye level.

"Welcome home, Daisy," she said, smiling.

Chapter Four

On Monday afternoon, dark clouds began to build in the sky and thunder rumbled in the distance. Ted and Ryan were parked in the patrol car in plain view at the side of an elementary school.

The boisterous children were getting out for the day and the street was lined with yellow buses and parents in cars. The silent presence of the police kept traffic at the proper speed.

"Man, those kids have a lot of energy," Ted said. "We should be that good after a day's work."

"Feeling your age today, Sharpe?" Ryan said, chuckling. "I've tried to warn you that the party life would catch up with you, but you weren't having any of my worldly wisdom. Big weekend, huh?"

Ted shot a glare at his partner, then redirected his attention to the slow-moving, congested traffic in front of the school.

"No, MacAllister," he said. "I did *not* have a big weekend."

"Why not?"

Ted shrugged. "I wasn't in the mood." He paused. "Do you think I'm too young for a mid-life crisis?"

"Beats me. I don't think every guy has one. You know, it's not a given, like women going through the change of life. Then again, there are some experts who say men definitely have a sort of mid-life-change thing, too. Hell, I really don't know."

"You're a lot of help."

"Why the question?"

"It's not that big a deal. It's just that lately I've felt restless, kind of edgy. In the past, I never had trouble filling idle hours. In fact, I didn't seem to have enough time to do everything I wanted to. Now? I'm flat, dulled-out. I decide to do something, then realize I really don't want to. It's weird."

"Not good, buddy," Ryan answered. "It sounds like how I felt toward the end of owning MacAllister Security Systems. I have to give you credit, though, for being in touch with yourself and knowing something is off-kilter. I denied it far longer than I should have."

"Yeah, well, it turned out all right. You're back where you belong, being a cop."

"You're not getting bored on the force, are you?"

"No, no, the job is fine," Ted reassured him. "No problem there. It's my leisure time that's suddenly tripping me up."

"You seemed okay at the mall when we were getting Teddy's dog. Scooter is nuts, by the way. She bounces like a pogo stick when she's excited about something. She goes straight up in the air. Teddy thinks she's great. I've never seen a dog bounce like that."

Ted chuckled as he envisioned the bouncing beagle.

"Anyway, back at the mall," Ryan said, "you were loose, relaxed, your usual self. Or were you faking it?"

"No, I enjoyed myself. Before you called, though, I was pacing the floor."

"And after you went home?"

"I had a good time at Hannah's because of Daisy but—" Ted stopped speaking and inwardly groaned.

Damn, he'd had no intention of revealing the fact that he'd bought a kitten for Hannah. Ryan would razz him to no end, he just knew it. He'd make a simple thing like buying a new neighbor a welcoming gift into a major man-woman event. Oh, hell, Ted didn't need the hassle he was about to get.

"Hannah is your new neighbor, Ms. Doodle," Ryan said. "But who's Daisy?"

"The kitten I bought Hannah at the mall after you left," Ted said. *Gear up, Sharpe. Here it comes.*

"Oh."

A few seconds ticked by, then a few more, but Ryan kept silent.

"Okay, MacAllister," Ted said. "Spit it out before you blow a fuse."

Ryan glanced over at him. "Spit what out?"

"I bought Hannah a kitten. Okay? Fine. What would you expect me to do? Bake her a cake? She was having a problem feeling like the apartment was home. You know what I mean? I figured the kitten would be there, greet her, be company for her, make the place more homey."

"Oh."

"She was really tickled with the kitten. She got tears in her eyes, but said pregnant women are very emotional. A volleyball is five months along, by the way. Her baby is due New Year's Day."

Ryan nodded. "Oh."

"She named the kitten Daisy to represent the daffodils-and-daisies theory her gran taught her. Her grandmother raised her because her parents were killed when she was three. Whenever Hannah was bummed, her gran would say that tomorrow would be sunny and bring her daffodils and daisies. Nice, huh?"

"Yeah."

"So she named the kitten Daisy because she felt the little bugger would make her days sunnier, and make the apartment seem more like a home. I called it exactly right and I was glad, I really was. Hannah just lit up and her eyes sparkled. There. That's it. Don't make a big deal out of it."

"Okay."

Ted drummed the fingers of one hand on his knee. "You're getting on my nerves, MacAllister."

Ryan swallowed a burst of laughter, then stiffened. "Heads up. That joker is going at least thirty-five in a fifteen."

Ryan started the engine, turned on the lights and siren and pulled out into the street in pursuit of the speeding vehicle.

That evening after Teddy was in bed, Ryan related the story of Hannah and Daisy to Deedee. Rain pelted the windows and thunder roared across the heavens.

"Very interesting," Deedee said, tapping one fingertip against her chin. "Ted was defensive about buying the kitten for Hannah?"

"Like a hostile witness on the stand. I really got under his skin because I reacted as though he were talking about the weather. Ready for this? Ted thinks he might be having a mid-life crisis."

"Oh, dear," she said, smiling. "What he's having is an attraction to a lady who is far removed from the type of woman with whom he usually associates. Oh, Ryan, his buying Hannah that kitten is the sweetest thing. And I adore the daffodils-and-daisies story. Hannah sounds like she's absolutely lovely."

"Well, I wouldn't mention any of this to Ted if I were you. He's very touchy about the subject of Hannah Johnson, aka Ms. Doodle."

"You'd better keep me posted on all of this, Ryan MacAllister."

"I will, but if I come home strangled, it's because Officer Theodore Sharpe is a tad hard to live with right now."

"Oh, you poor baby," she said, slipping onto his lap. "Do you need some tender loving care?"

"Yes, ma'am," he said, wrapping his arms around her. "A whole lot of TLC."

Ryan captured Deedee's lips with his. No more words were spoken for a long, long time.

Ted sat in front of the long table that covered one wall of the second bedroom in his apartment. As he slowly and carefully sanded one of the minuscule rungs that would be part of the miniature cradle he was making, he hummed along with the country-western music playing on the stereo in the living room.

On the opposite wall was a glass-fronted cabinet which held about two dozen small pieces of furniture he'd made over the past months.

A bookcase next to it contained tools, brushes, a variety of paints and stains and several stacks of woodworking books and magazines.

Earlier in the evening, he'd begun reading the latest book he'd purchased at Deedee's store, an instruction manual for constructing a dollhouse.

As Ted worked, he smiled, realizing that if he built the house and eventually filled it with handcrafted furniture, it would never leave this room.

Nope, he thought. One furnished dollhouse wouldn't cut it when he considered how many little MacAllister girls there were.

And what about the boys? They'd expect something made especially for them by their uncle Ted, too. No, the dollhouse and furniture would remain right there. He'd give the MacAllister munchkins visitation rights.

His smiled faded and he sighed.

Uncle Ted. Ted Sharpe, Professional Uncle Extraordinaire, that's who he was. Not a father, just an uncle. Not an everyday part of those kids' lives, just a drop-in entity. Out of sight, out of mind. And all the MacAllisters assumed that was the way he wanted it.

Damn it, Sharpe, he admonished himself. *Knock it off.* His life was structured just fine the way it was. He had the best of both worlds; the family scene when the mood struck, the singles scene the remainder of the time.

He came and went as he pleased, and had no major responsibilities, no worries or woes. He was sitting pretty, doing great.

Or so he'd believed until the last week or so.

He'd been off the mark, feeling weird, strange, not like himself at all. Restless, edgy, wired, he couldn't get a handle on what was wrong.

It was like . . . yeah, like people who came home, moved through their house and didn't realize for an hour or more that the television had been ripped off. They were so used to it being there, that it took a while for it to sink in that it was missing.

Missing.

Ted set the sandpaper and cradle rung on the table and stared into space.

Missing. Something was missing from his life, his day-to-day existence. Well, hell, what a lousy conclusion to come to as to why he was out of sorts. His life as it stood had suited him just dandy for many years.

Why would it suddenly seem as if something was missing?

If this was his mid-life crisis, Ted sure as hell hoped it wouldn't last long. He wasn't accustomed to being bummed-out, mentally listless, physically dragging through the days, tossing and turning at night.

Uncle Ted.

No, damn it, not being married, not having children, was *not* the source of his dilemma.

Ted got to his feet and left the room, smacking the light switch off as he passed. Shoving his hands into the back pockets of his faded jeans, he wandered around the living room, a frown on his face. In the background, Vince Gill crooned about loneliness.

Okay, Sharpe, get it together, he told himself. *Analyze the situation.*

He was single. He liked it that way. He had kids who clambered all over him whenever he visited them. That was the end of *that* story.

Women. He had plenty of women to pick from... every age, shape, size, career and IQ imaginable. Plenty of women. Check. No problem.

Career. Set. A-OK. He was doing exactly what he wanted to do. And he was a damn good cop.

Friends. He had great friends, true and loyal friends.

Money. No sweat. He lived well, had a healthy retirement portfolio growing steadily and didn't do without anything he really wished to have.

"So what in the hell is missing?" he said aloud, pulling his hands free and flinging out his arms.

Before the discussion between Ted and Ted could continue, a boom of thunder crashed overhead and in the next moment the lights went out.

"Well, hell," Ted said.

He stood statue-still, planting his hands on his hips as he waited for his eyes to adapt to the inky darkness. When he could see well enough to move, he made his way into the kitchen and retrieved a flashlight from the drawer designated for odds and ends.

With the bright beam of light ahead of him, he went to the sofa, slouched onto it and flicked off the flashlight. In the next instant, he turned it back on and lunged to his feet.

Ms. Doodle, he thought. Did Hannah have a flashlight? Candles? Had that extremely loud thunder frightened her?

Could she remember where all her furniture was placed so she could find a flashlight, if she had one, without falling over something?

What if she hurt herself? Or the baby? Or stepped on Daisy and smashed the kitten flat?

Hannah could be in trouble over there! Ted realized. He'd better go find out if she was all right. Yes, it was his duty as a police officer to leap into action in a single bound at the slightest hint of potential disaster or possible danger.

"Sharpe, you're so corny," he said, shaking his head in self-disgust. "Just shut up and go see if Hannah is okay."

The hallway was pitch-black and Ted's flashlight cast eerie shadows beyond its bright circle of light. The thunder continued to rumble and roar as it rolled across the sky.

At Hannah's apartment, he knocked sharply.

"Hannah?" he called. "It's Ted."

Nothing.

He leaned his ear against the door, silently cursing the noisy thunder. Straightening, he pounded his fist on the door.

"Hannah?"

Nothing.

Ted's heart began to race, as well as his imagination.

Why didn't she answer? Was she hurt, unable to get to the door? He could kick in the door. Or maybe he should make his way down the back stairs to the ground floor, find the manager's apartment and drag the guy up here with the master key.

Yeah, he'd have to use the stairway because the elevator wouldn't be working.

Ted stiffened, beads of sweat dotting his forehead.

The elevator!

Lord, what if Hannah was stuck in the elevator?

Maybe she'd gone out to dinner with some of her teacher friends, saw the ominous clouds building in the sky and headed for home. Then the storm broke before she arrived at the complex, and she hurried inside but was already drenched as she entered the elevator. Halfway to the fourth floor...*blam*...no electricity...!

Hannah could be cold and wet, held captive in a dark cage...terrified!

He had to call the police!

"Damn it," Ted said. "I *am* the police."

Sharpe, slow down, he ordered himself. He wasn't behaving to form at all. He didn't usually go off the deep end, panic, automatically think the worst.

He was an in-control officer of the law who approached each new situation he encountered with a swift and analytical appraisal of what needed to be done.

Ted splayed one hand on his heart, took a deep, steadying breath and let it out slowly.

There. He was fine now calm, cool and collected. Right? Right.

In the next instant Ted began to beat on Hannah's door again with his fist.

"Hannah! Hannah, are you in there? It's Ted. Say something. Anything. Speak to me."

"Ted?" came a muffled reply.

"Oh, thank God." He leaned his forehead against the door.

"Ted?"

He lifted his head. "Yeah, I'm here. Can you get to the door?"

"I'm trying to, but...*ow!*"

"Ow?" he yelled. "Why ow?" What happened? Are you hurt?"

He heard the faint sound of the safety chain rattling, then the lock being unsnapped. The door was opened slowly, no more than three inches. Ted raised the flashlight and saw Hannah's tilted head, giving him a rather lopsided view of her eyes.

"Let me in," he said.

"Lower the flashlight."

"What?"

"Ted, I'd just gotten out of the shower when the lights went out. I'm wrapped in a towel. I made my way to the linen cupboard where I'd put the flash-light, but the batteries were dead.''

"Oh."

"I have candles in the kitchen drawer, but I've stubbed my toe twice already trying to get there. I'd really appreciate your finding my candles for me, but could you shine the light on the floor, please? I'm not exactly dressed to receive company."

"Oh. Sure."

Ted did as instructed with the beam of light as he entered the apartment, deciding absently that Hannah had cute toes as he directed the light on her feet.

She closed the door and locked it.

"I'm so glad you're here," she said, her voice trembling slightly. "Thank you for thinking of me. I'm being childish, I know, but it was so dark and I was bumping into things and..."

"Ah, Hannah," he said. "I was so damn worried about you."

Before he realized he was moving, Ted wrapped his arms around Hannah and pulled her close, feeling the damp towel and the slope of her stomach. The beam of light was directed toward the ceiling.

Hannah encircled his waist with her arms and leaned her head on his chest, the towel tucked into it-self between her breasts.

Ted inhaled her aroma of flowers and soap, savor-ing it. He was acutely aware of her breasts pressing against his chest and felt a hot surge of heat low in his body.

Hannah's protruding stomach, with her baby was safely nestled inside, was, to his startled amazement,

extremely sensuous. She was the epitome of womanliness, of femininity.

Ah, Hannah, his mind hummed. She was safe,
nothing had happened to her, she was all right. Ted
was holding her fast and wasn't going to let her go. He
would protect her from harm. She was so fragile, delicate and vulnerable... and so was her precious baby.
And the part of Hannah that was pure woman was
sending Ted up in flames of desire.

Hannah closed her eyes, relishing the strength of
Ted's powerful body. He was so strong, so masculine, so... so there.

She'd been frightened, afraid she'd fall over a piece
of furniture and hurt the baby. Icy fear had clutched
her heart, causing unshed tears to sting her eyes and
close her throat. She'd been so alone in the dark, so
terribly alone.

But now Ted was here.

For this stolen moment out of time, she was going
to allow herself the luxury of leaning on him, of gathering inner fortitude from a source other than herself.

During the weeks, months, years ahead, there would
be no one there for her to turn to. She'd raise her child
to the best of her ability, cope with crises as they came,
greet each new day with the daffodils-and-daisies outlook taught to her by her beloved gran.

But now, right now, Hannah was so very tired, both
physically and emotionally. The fright she'd experienced in the suddenly dark apartment had drained her.

But Ted was here, holding her in an embrace that
was like a cocoon; a comforting warmth like a soft

blanket. She was safe. Ted represented a solid shield between her and the reality of her life.

It felt so good, so right . . . just for a moment.

Hannah sighed and Ted's arms tightened around her slightly. She pressed more firmly against him, filling the essence of herself with his strength that seemed to flow into her, giving her what she so desperately needed to carry on, to stand alone.

But then . . . slowly, slowly something began to stir deep within her. A tiny whisper of heat, like a glowing ember, was burning brighter, hotter, causing passion to heighten and thrum through her.

Hannah was so incredibly *aware* of her own body and the exquisite feel of it being molded to Ted's. Her breasts were crushed to the hard wall of his chest, yet the pain was sweet, an affirmation of her femininity compared to his rugged masculinity. The baby inside her was not a barrier between her and Ted, it was a precious connection, touching them both, its very existence meshing them into one entity.

Oh, dear heaven, Hannah thought, she was awash with desire, wanting Ted.

Hannah, don't, her mind yelled. This was wrong, terribly wrong. She had to move away from Ted, borrow the flashlight so she could get to the bedroom and put on some clothes. She had to regain her sense of reason, her sense of self. *Now.*

Hannah shifted and tilted her head back to look up at Ted. The shadowy luminescence of the flashlight made it possible for her to see him, not clearly, but enough to be able to meet his gaze.

"Ted, I..." She stopped speaking, hating the thread of desire-induced breathlessness in her voice.

"Hannah."

That was all he said, just her name, spoken in a voice gritty with smoldering passion.

Hannah's breath caught and rational thought fled into oblivion.

Ah, Hannah, Ted's hazy mind echoed.

Then he lowered his head and kissed her.

Chapter Five

The kiss was soft and gentle, tentative at first. But then it deepened, becoming intense and urgent as the licking flames of desire within Hannah and Ted leaped higher, consuming them.

The flashlight slipped from Ted's hand to land with a quiet thud on the carpet. The light created a glowing circle around them. It was as though nothing existed beyond that sphere. They were in a place that was meant only for them, and passions soared.

Ted drank of the taste of Hannah, his tongue delving into her mouth to seek and find her tongue. His arousal was heavy, aching with the want of her as his hands roamed over the damp towel, then up to the velvet softness of her dewy skin. His heart thundered and a groan rumbled deep in his chest.

Hannah returned the kiss in total abandon, filling her senses with the taste, the aroma, the feel of Ted. She splayed her hands on his back, relishing the taut muscles that bunched and moved beneath her palms.

She felt alive, so incredibly alive, and inwardly rejoiced in her own womanliness that was a counterpart to Ted's wondrous masculinity.

Ted lifted his head to draw a rough breath, then slanted his mouth in the other direction, capturing Hannah's lips once again.

Hannah, his mind hummed. *Hannah.* He wanted her with a raging need far greater than anything he'd experienced before. Emotions of protectiveness and possessiveness slammed against his mind, intertwining with heated desire.

He felt as though he'd been lifted up and away from the world as he knew it, and transported into a hazy mist that belonged to him and to Hannah, with no one else allowed to intrude.

It was magical.

It was theirs.

Again Ted raised his head a fraction of an inch, speaking close to her lips.

"Hannah," he said, his voice raspy, "I want you. Hannah?"

"Yes," she whispered. "Oh, yes. I want you too, Ted. I've never felt so..."

Suddenly, the baby shifted, rolled, then delivered a swift kick. Hannah blinked as she was jarringly returned to reality. She stiffened in Ted's arms.

"Dear heaven," Hannah said. "What am I doing?"

"Kissing me, wanting me," he said. "I want to make love with you, Hannah."

She wiggled out of his arms, clutching the towel with both hands where it was tucked between her breasts.

"No, no," she said, shaking her head. "I can't do this." She took another step backward. "I'm sorry if I led you to believe that I... Oh, my God, I can imagine what you must think of me."

"I think," he said quietly, willing his body back under control, "that you're a very desirable woman who isn't afraid to acknowledge her own sexuality. I think, I know, you want me as much as I want you. There's nothing wrong with that, Hannah. We're adults, free to make our own choices."

"This adult," she said, her voice rising, "is pregnant, in case you didn't notice."

"We wouldn't hurt the baby. I asked Ryan about that when Deedee was pregnant. I just wondered, you know, so I asked him."

"That's not the point. What kind of person leaps into a man's arms when she's pregnant with another man's child? I'm...I'm a wanton woman."

Ted chuckled, then dragged a restless hand through his hair.

"No, you're not," he said, smiling. "Wanton woman? I can't believe you actually said that. Look, you're a normal, healthy woman in touch with herself, with her wants and needs. There's nothing to get upset about."

"Oh, ha! I'm standing here in nothing more than a skimpy towel, pregnant as a volleyball, to quote your eloquent description, flinging myself at a man I hardly know. That, Mr. Sharpe, is disgusting.''

"No. It's delightful, real and right, Ms. Doodle."

"Oh-h-h, there's no talking to you." She leaned down and picked up the flashlight. "I'm going to get dressed. Then I'll find my candles, give you back your flashlight and see you out. I'd appreciate it if you'd forget that this incident took place."

"Can't."

"Why not?"

Ted shrugged. "It's imprinted on my brain with indelible memory ink. Besides, why would I want to forget it? Kissing you was fantastic, Hannah Johnson. I may have to go home and stand under a cold shower for an hour, but it'll be worth it. Oh, yes ma'am, holding you, kissing you, your kissing me, was sensational, really something."

"Oh, well, fancy that." Hannah smiled, but in the next second frowned. "No, no, no. I don't want to discuss this. *I'm* going to forget it happened."

She moved past him and started toward the bedroom, shining the flashlight ahead of her.

"Hannah."

She stopped, her back to Ted.

"What?" she said, a sharp edge to her voice.

"It won't work, you know. Kisses like the ones we shared can't be dusted off that easily. Give it your best shot if it will make you feel better, but you're wasting your time. You *will* remember, Hannah."

"Shut up, Sharpe."

Hannah marched from the room to the accompaniment of Ted's soft laughter.

He watched the light disappear, then turned, making his way carefully to the kitchen in search of the candles. He found a drawer, opened it and rummaged around in the dark hole. His fingers closed around two taper candles. Further exploring produced two square, wooden holders and a book of matches.

After lighting one of the candles, he returned to the living room, sat down on the sofa, lit the other candle and placed both lighted candles on the coffee table.

Daisy appeared out of nowhere and crawled up onto the sofa.

"Hi, Daisy," Ted said, patting the kitten on the head. "How's life?"

He sank back against the puffy cushions.

Life? he thought. Life was strange, very weird. If someone would have told him that he'd soon be kissing a volleyball-size pregnant woman in a room with no electricity because of a storm, he'd have told that idiot to give it up and ship himself to the farm.

But not only was that insane statement true, it went further than that. Kissing said person had been, without a doubt, dynamite. Man, oh, man, he'd been on fire. He had wanted Hannah so badly he ached.

And the maze of emotions? They'd been tumbling through his mind so fast, he couldn't even decipher all of them. *That* had never happened to him before. *But* he'd never spent time with a woman like Ms. Doodle before, either.

She was very, very different from the women he associated with.

"No joke, fool," he muttered. "She's pregnant. That is definitely different."

Ted frowned and shook his head.

No, that wasn't it...the fact that Hannah was pregnant. There was no ignoring that she was going to have a baby, but it wasn't a turnoff, not by a long shot. It made her seem very feminine, womanly, very appealing. And it caused him to feel extremely masculine and protective, like a knight prepared to slay the dragon.

As for the man who had fathered her child? Forget him, Ted cautioned, he was worthless. The baby is Hannah's, pure and simple.

Hannah...a charming combination of stand-on-her-own-two-feet strength and independence, and needing-protection-vulnerability. She'd looked him square in the eye and told him he was a rude, unpleasant man, then she'd wept at the sight of a furry little kitten.

There was a childlike innocence about her at times, yet when she allowed her sexuality to surface, she was one-hundred-percent woman.

Oh, Ted decided, she was something, all right, Ms. Hannah Johnson. That was firmly established, a given. The question that was driving him nuts was why he, Theodore Sharpe, was attracted to her? She wasn't even remotely close to being his type.

"I'm losing it, Daisy," he said to the kitten. "My mid-life crisis is scrambling my gray matter. Sad, huh? Yeah, I knew you'd agree with me."

The flashlight beam shone across the floor as Hannah returned to the living room. She came to the sofa, turned off the light and extended the flashlight to Ted.

He took it without really looking at it, his gaze riveted on Hannah.

She was wearing a rose-colored, velour robe that fell to the floor in soft folds and had long, full sleeves. It zipped up the front, in one long enticing line that caused Ted's fingertips to tingle at the thought of slowly, so very slowly, inching that zipper downward.

The candlelight cast a glow over her, and once again she looked like a lovely cameo, delicate and beautiful beyond measure.

Oh, man, how he wanted this woman, Ted thought.

"Thank you for coming here, Ted," Hannah said quietly. "I appreciate your concern. It was very... neighborly of you."

Ted patted the sofa cushion next to him.

"Sit down, Hannah," he said. "Please?"

"No."

He frowned. "Hey, I'm not going to seduce you, for Pete's sake. I just want to talk to you for a minute or two."

"Two. Maximum."

She sat down on the far end of the sofa and smoothed the robe over her stomach before turning to look at Ted.

What candlelight did for Ted Sharpe's rugged features and sun-streaked hair, she thought, was sinful. It should be declared against the law and he should arrest himself.

Ted, Hannah thought. She'd lectured herself firmly and at great length while she was in the bedroom. What had happened with Ted, those exquisite kisses shared with Ted, the intense desire she'd felt for Ted, the burning want and need, were now erased from her memory bank.

Well, that was stretching the truth a tad. She *would* forget what had transpired once Ted left the apartment and she was alone. The mere presence of the man was enough to cause the desire still simmering within her to be fanned hotter and hotter.

"Two minutes, remember?" she said.

Ted scooted closer to her, nearly squashing Daisy in the process. The kitten jumped to the floor and dashed away.

"I can hear you from the other end of the sofa, Ted," Hannah said, lifting her chin.

"It's my two minutes. You didn't put any distance restrictions on it."

"Mmm."

He slid one arm across the top of the sofa behind her, being careful not to touch her, then shifted slightly to look directly at her.

"Hannah," he said, "what happened here tonight wasn't wrong. It wasn't something to regret. It was honest and real, and equally shared. There was nothing 'wanton,' to use your quaint word, about it. I really hate knowing you're upset over it."

Hannah sighed. "Yes, all right, I'll admit I was being rather dramatic with my 'wanton woman' spiel. And, yes, I'll take responsibility for my half of it. The thing is, Ted, that nothing like that neither should, nor will, happen again."

"Why not?"

"Because I'm not free to engage in . . . to allow myself to . . . you know what I mean."

"You're free. You're divorced. You're a single woman. If you're referring to being pregnant, you're off base. That baby is a part of you, a lovely part."

She smiled slightly. "Cute as a volleyball."

"You're the cutest volleyball I've ever seen."

"Ted, listen to me," she said, her smile gone. "I'm not *emotionally* free."

"You're still in love with and loyal to your ex-husband?"

"No, no, no. You see, he wasn't who I thought he was or who I believed him to be. When I told him I was pregnant, his true colors came to light. I had to choose, he said, between him and the baby because he wanted no part of raising a child. I went to Nevada and obtained a quick and quiet divorce."

Ted muttered a very earthy expletive.

"I'm obviously not capable of seeing a man as he truly is. I buy into the facade, trust far too easily. It's a flaw, a major flaw of mine. That's what I mean when I say I'm not emotionally free. I'm held captive by my inability to tell the good guys from the bad."

"Based on one mistake? Hannah, come on, that's not fair."

"No, not *one*. I dated a boy in high school for two years. He said he loved me, respected me, the whole nine yards. It turned out he was telling his friends that we had sex all the time. It wasn't true. He wasn't who I believed him to be."

"He was a kid."

"He was my choice. The first year of college, I went out with a football player. Guess what? He had a pregnant wife back in Oklahoma. Then a year or so later, I met the man I married. His name is Maxwell. He was ten years older than me, had a thriving insurance company and said he'd postponed marriage until he was financially stable.''

''Maxwell? Anyone with a name like that is definitely a dud. Did he use 'Max'?''

''No. Maxwell, always Maxwell.''

''A dud.''

''He was wonderful... I thought. He was mature and considerate, took me to nice places, treated me like I was so special. He had a house that he said would never be a real home until I married him and lived there.''

''And you did.''

''Yes. I was so happy. Everything was glorious until I discovered I was pregnant. Then the real Maxwell surfaced and I had to face my flaw again. I had made a horrible mistake...trusted and believed in the wrong man... again. I will not *ever* put myself in that position in the future... waiting, waiting, waiting, to find out who a man proves to *really* be.''

''Whew,'' Ted said. ''I'm sorry you've had so much heartache, Hannah, I truly am. But you're giving the whole male populace a bum rap. Some of us are the real goods, you know.''

''Oh, yes, of course I know that, but *I* can't decipher one from the next. I just don't know how. I refuse to run the risk of attempting to unravel that puzzle again.''

''Hannah, I'm a nice guy!'' Ted said, nearly yelling.

"Maybe." She shrugged. "Maybe not. *I* don't intend to find out." She folded her hands on top of her protruding stomach and smiled at him pleasantly. "Well, there you have it, neat and tidy, the story of my life."

Ted leaned toward her. "How can you be so calm? You recited all that like someone reading off their grocery list."

"Because I'm tired of crying, Ted," she said, serious again. "Entering into a relationship with a man is guaranteed heartbreak for me. I've accepted that. As the psychologists say, 'I own it.' Since I've acknowledged it, I can forgive myself for my glitch."

She pointed one finger in the air.

"However," she went on, "having faced the situation as it stands, I can no longer make excuses or place the blame on anyone but myself. I must proceed with at least a modicum of maturity and realize that a serious relationship is not territory in which I am equipped to travel. So I won't. Not ever."

She nodded decisively and patted her stomach.

"My baby and I will do just fine together. We'll be Mommy, Baby and Daisy. How's that?"

"It stinks," Ted said, frowning.

"It certainly does not. We'll be The Terrific Trio. That title is in capital letters." She paused. "I took a cash settlement at the time of my divorce, having decided I wished to have no part of monthly child-support payments from a man who wanted nothing to do with the child.

"Maxwell signed papers saying he would make no claim on this baby, nor attempt to see it or interact with it in the future. One of my friends told me that he's already engaged to a nineteen-year-old girl who wants to be an actress.''

"Dandy," Ted said, rolling his eyes heavenward.

"So, if I live on a tight budget and give private piano lessons, which I'm doing, I should be all right during this year off from teaching. I'm trying to have my students practice quietly when they're here so they won't disturb you, especially if they're playing 'Yankee Doodle.'"

"Oh, man," Ted said, getting to his feet. He started forward, immediately whacking his shin on the edge of the coffee table. "Ow! Damn it, that hurt."

He moved around the table and began to pace the floor in front of the table, back and forth, back and forth.

Hannah watched him, feeling as though she were at a tennis match.

"Not good," Ted said, continuing his trek. "This is not good at all. You're too young to have set a program into place for the rest of your life, especially one this drastic, restricting, narrow."

"Realistic," Hannah added.

Ted stopped, planted his hands on his hips and glared at her. "Try this on for size, Ms. Doodle. Are you going to raise your child with this crummy philosophy? Teach him, or her, not to trust their own judgment when picking their life's partner?"

"Of course not. This isn't a genetic flaw, for crying out loud. It's mine alone and has nothing to do with the baby. I know my personal limitations and will conduct myself accordingly in the future."

"You're so wrong, it's a crime."

"So arrest me, Officer Sharpe."

"Don't tempt me. If I thought it might make you come to your senses, I'd toss you in the clink."

"That," Hannah said, laughing, "was funny."

Before Ted could retort, the lights flickered, went out, then came on full force. Hannah blinked against the sudden brightness, then leaned forward and blew out the candles.

Daisy bounded into the room, crawled up the arm of the sofa, perched there and began to methodically wash a paw.

"Let there be light," Hannah said, flinging out her arms. "End of crisis."

"Not even close. *You* are a walking, talking crisis. Hannah, what about the daffodils-and-daisies theory your gran taught you?"

"Oh, how sweet of you to remember my telling you that. Thank you."

"You're welcome. Answer the question."

"It's perfectly clear, Ted. In order to have sunny tomorrows with daffodils and daisies, I must steer clear of what I know to be a danger zone. That is just plain, old-fashioned common sense. I'm implementing Gran's theory extremely well."

"You're an exasperating woman at times, do you know that? My mid-life crisis is tough enough to handle without having to deal with this cockeyed program of yours."

Hannah's eyes widened. "My stars, you're having a mid-life crisis? Aren't you rather young for that?"

"At thirty-four? Yeah, I think I am, but there's no other explanation for the way I've been feeling."

"Such as?"

"Restless, edgy, wired. My leisure time is the pits all of a sudden, and I—" He stopped speaking and sliced one hand through the air. "Cut. You're tricky, Ms. Doodle, very clever, but it didn't work. We're discussing you here, not me."

"Actually, this discussion is finished because I'm exhausted and I'm going to bed." She got to her feet. "I want to thank you again for coming over when the electricity went out. It was very kind and thoughtful of you. I'll buy some batteries for my flashlight so I'll be properly prepared in the future."

"Well, keep my flashlight in the meantime. I have another one." He started toward the door. "I'll get out of here and let you get some sleep."

Hannah followed him to the door. Ted opened it, then turned to look at her.

"And the discussion is *not* finished." He brushed a kiss over her lips. "Good night, Hannah."

"Good night, Ted," she said softly.

He left the apartment and Hannah locked the door behind him. She stood statue-still for a moment, the fingertips of one hand floating upward to rest on her lips.

"Forget it," she said aloud. "Come on, Daisy. It's time for bed."

The next evening, Ted, Deedee and Ryan sat at a round table on the MacAllisters' deck, enjoying dinner.

Teddy was already in bed for the night, having refused to take an afternoon nap. The tired baby had been more than ready to be tucked into his crib shortly after Ted had arrived.

Scooter the beagle was planted firmly across Ryan's feet.

"Why does she do that?" Ryan said, peering under the table. "Every time I sit down, she flops onto my feet. When I move or get up, she's disturbed, then does it all over again."

"Maybe she has a foot fetish," Ted said.

"Only for Ryan's feet," Deedee said, laughing. "She doesn't do it to anyone else."

"Lucky me," Ryan said dryly. "I can't tell you how thrilled I am."

"Have some more pizza, honey," Deedee said. "Just pretend she's not there." She reached for a slice for herself. "Super-Duper Pizza Supreme Deluxe Extraordinaire. Mmm, delicious. I'm so glad Jillian introduced us to this delight from Mario's. It was awfully nice of you to bring it, Ted."

"It's a bribe," he said, taking another slice. "I need the two of you to give me some advice."

"Really?" Ryan said. "We were together the entire day, Sharpe, and you didn't tap into my genius-level brain."

"Because," he said, glaring at Ryan, "you're not a woman."

"He certainly isn't," Deedee said, batting her eyelashes at her husband. "And I can't begin to tell you how pleased I am about that fact."

"Could we get serious here, people?" Ted said.

"I told you he was hard to live with, Deedee," Ryan said. "I may have to shoot him to put him out of his mid-life-crisis misery and save my own sanity."

"Hush, Ryan," she said. "Ted is, even as we speak, contemplating punching you in the nose."

"Oh. Okay, Theodore, you have the floor."

"I don't want to talk about my mid-life crisis," Ted said, frowning. "The subject matter is Hannah."

"Ms. Doodle?" Deedee said.

"Yeah. Now then, listen up."

Ted related the conversation he'd had with Hannah the previous evening, omitting the fact that he'd kissed her. He also failed to mention that he'd spent the night tossing and turning, due to his body aching with desire.

"Goodness," Deedee said when Ted stopped speaking. "Let me sum this up, to be certain I understand it all correctly."

"Whatever," Ted muttered.

"Hannah Johnson," Deedee said, staring into space, "believes she is unable to properly perceive the true nature of a man. Her choices in the past have been wrong, because the men were never who she believed them to be."

Ted nodded. "Yup."

"Therefore," Deedee went on, "she's determined to never again become seriously involved with a man. She's very calm about her conclusion, has moved past the pain of being hurt time and again and now presents the philosophy for her entire future as calmly as she might report on the weather. Right?"

"That's it in a nutshell," Ted said.

"Okay," Ryan said. "But what are we supposed to give you advice about?"

"You're so dense, MacAllister," Ted said. "Read my lips. How do I convince Hannah that she's making a terrible mistake? She's sentencing herself to a life alone for no reason. So, yeah, she picked some duds, including her husband, but there *are* nice guys in this world."

"Like you?" Deedee said.

"No, Deedee, not like me." Ted paused. "I mean, I consider myself a nice guy, but that's beside the point. I'm not attempting to get her to trust and believe in *me,* or have a relationship with *me.* I just think I should convince her to chuck her lousy philosophy, and keep an open mind about men in general, so she doesn't miss out on the happiness she deserves to have."

"Oh-h-h, I see," Deedee said. "That makes sense."

"It does?" Ryan said.

Deedee patted his hand. "Trust me. It does."

"Why do you consider this *your* mission to undertake?" Ryan asked Ted.

"Because I'm a nice guy, remember?" he said, nearly shouting.

"Stay calm, gentlemen," Deedee said. "Ted, I'm very impressed by your noble intentions."

"Oh, brother," Ryan said, rolling his eyes heavenward.

"Hush, Ryan," Deedee said. "Ted, the first order of business is for us to meet Hannah. It's extremely difficult to give you advice about a person we know in name only. Why don't the four of us go out to dinner

Saturday night? We'll pick a place that isn't too fancy, but quiet enough to chat easily.''

"What am I supposed to say to her?" Ted said. " 'Hey, Hannah, want to go out to dinner so Dee-dee...forget about Ryan being any help...can gather data on you, and formulate a plan I can use to straighten out your wacko thinking?' Give me a break.''

"No, idiot," Ryan said. "You say that as her friendly neighbor it has occurred to you that you know some terrific people she might like to meet, so how about going out to dinner with you and them?''

"Ryan MacAllister," Deedee said, "that's marvel-ous.'' She narrowed her eyes. "When did you become such a slick operator?''

He grinned at her. "I have hidden talents.''

"Mmm," she said, raising one eyebrow.

"Well," Ted said, "I could try that approach, I guess. I'll let you know how it goes." He looked at Ryan. "Terrific people?''

"Terrific," Ryan repeated decisively, then his eyes widened. "Oh, hell.''

"What's wrong?" Deedee said.

"Scooter just wet on my shoes!''

Deedee and Ted dissolved in laughter.

After Ted left, Deedee and Ryan remained on the deck, watching the stars appear like sparkling dia-monds on black velvet.

"Hannah Johnson," Deedee said finally, breaking the comfortable silence.

"I told you Ted was acting weird. Some people get hooked on saving the whales. Sharpe is determined to save Ms. Doodle... from herself."

"Tsk, tsk," Deedee said. "You didn't see the forest for the tree in front of your nose."

"Huh?"

"Honey, remember when I said that Ted was attracted to Hannah? What he doesn't realize yet is that he's on this campaign *for himself*. He wants to change Hannah's philosophy so she'll give *him* a chance to be an important part of her life."

"He does?"

"Yes, my sweet, he most certainly does."

"Well," Hannah said, "I don't know, Ted."

"Hey, Deedee and Ryan are *terrific* people," Ted assured her. "Wouldn't you like to make some new friends?"

"They're the ones who are parents to your godson, Teddy?"

"Yes."

"That would be nice. You know... to talk to the mother of a baby. My teacher friends don't have any children."

"It's settled then. We'll all go out to dinner Saturday night to a casual but quiet restaurant. I'll pick you up at seven o'clock."

Chapter Six

On Saturday evening, Hannah sat at the piano playing *Claire de Lune,* willing the lovely melody to soothe her jangled nerves.

She did *not* want to go to dinner with Ted and his *terrific* friends. Why she had accepted the invitation, she had no idea.

She was going to feel like a bug under a microscope the entire evening, she just knew it.

Ted Sharpe, Mr. Swinging Bachelor of the Decade, was going to parade a pregnant, divorced woman in front of Deedee and Ryan MacAllister, instantly evoking their curiosity about her personal circumstances, *and* bringing to the front of their minds the question of what on earth a man like Ted was doing with the likes of her.

So, yes, all right, Ted's intentions had been admirable. He seemed very sincere about the conclusion he'd drawn that she might like to make new friends. The fact that Deedee and Ryan were parents of a baby held appeal, and she'd agreed to the proposal before thoroughly thinking it through.

She hadn't had one glimpse of Ted since he'd shown up at her door to present the plans for Saturday night.

On two occasions, she'd stood in the hallway fully prepared to march to his apartment and inform him that she'd changed her mind about the dinner date.

Both times, she'd decided she would sound like a childish idiot, and had rushed back into the safe haven of her living room.

Dinner date, her mind echoed. Dinner *date?* No, no, no, this was *not* a date in the usual sense of the word. She didn't have a *date* with Ted, swinging single that he was. That thought was really absurd. She didn't go out with men like him, whether she was pregnant or not.

No, this wasn't a date. It was a . . .

"Well, drat," she said, increasing the volume of her playing, "I don't know what this thing is, but I don't want to go."

Daisy managed to climb up one of the legs of the piano bench, then sat next to Hannah, giving the impression she'd arrived for the sole purpose of listening to the music.

Hannah smiled at the kitten, then continued to play, her fingers flying over the keys, pounding out *Claire de Lune* louder and louder.

*   *   *

A grin broke across Ted's face as he stood in front of the bathroom mirror to comb his hair.

Claire de Lune, he thought, was being played on the piano by Ms. Doodle at a volume that was probably being heard by the occupants of the apartment on the other side of her, as well as by those on the floor above and below.

Hannah certainly was an accomplished pianist, and the song was hauntingly beautiful. That, however, was beside the point. What *was* being telegraphed was the fact that Hannah was stressed, nervous about the evening ahead.

Ted nodded at his reflection, a smug expression on his face.

He'd known, just somehow known, that Hannah would get cold feet about the dinner date with him, Deedee and Ryan. He'd very carefully kept out of sight since issuing the invitation so she'd have no opportunity to cancel.

Each time he arrived at the apartment complex, he'd checked to see if her car was in the parking lot. If it was, he used the back stairs, to be certain she couldn't corner him in the elevator. He'd peer down the hall, then hightail it to his own apartment.

To wiggle out of going to dinner, Hannah would be forced to knock on his door, then present whatever lame excuse she'd manufactured. She might have considered doing exactly that, but he'd figured—and had been right—that she wouldn't have the courage to do it.

''You clever son-of-a-gun,'' he said to his image.

Ted left the bathroom, then shrugged into a gray sport coat that he wore over black trousers and a pale blue dress shirt open at the neck.

Without realizing he was doing it, he began to hum along with the music still reverberating through the wall. He shot the cuff of his shirt to check his watch, and realized he was ready to go far too early.

Wandering around the living room, he continued to hum as he straightened some magazines on the coffee table, then scooped a pile of junk mail off the sofa and dumped it in the trash.

In the kitchen, he put three glasses and two coffee mugs in the dishwasher, then wiped a blob of catsup off the counter.

As he surveyed the area for anything else needing his attention, he suddenly frowned.

Why was he spit-shining his apartment? He was admittedly a bit of a slob, and had never apologized to anyone for that fact. So, why was he fussing over a few dirty dishes and scattered mail?

It wasn't as though he was expecting company. He'd collect and deposit Hannah at her own place. She'd have no reason to be in *his*. Even if she *was* going to come in, he'd never worried about appearances when he'd brought other women in here.

Lord, was his mid-life crisis going to change him into a neatnick? What a disconcerting thought.

''Forget it,'' he said, starting across the room.

He had a dinner date with a lovely lady and two of his closest friends. Everyone would have a nice time. Deedee would get to know Hannah, and therefore be able to give him advice on how to tackle Ms. Doodle's ridiculous program for her future.

He left one lamp on, turned off another, went to the door and grabbed the knob.

Dinner date? he thought, not opening the door. As in, he had a *date* with Hannah Johnson to go out to dinner? Well, no, not really. Sort of. But not exactly. The evening ahead was set in motion so Deedee could accomplish a fact-finding mission regarding Hannah.

It wasn't a date, per se.

Well, yeah, okay, so he'd found himself looking forward to the event. Hell, he'd been in a better mood today than he'd enjoyed in quite a while.

Fine, that made sense. Hannah was an attractive, nice-to-be-with woman. Why shouldn't he be anticipating the pleasure of her company? Not, of course, that this was officially a date.

''Sharpe,'' he said aloud, shaking his head in self-disgust, ''get out of here before you think yourself to death.''

When Ted knocked on Hannah's door, the lilting music within the apartment stopped abruptly. A few moments later, Hannah opened the door.

''Hello, Ted,'' she said, not smiling. She stepped backward, her hand on the doorknob. ''Come in.''

Ted didn't move. When a sharp pain radiated across his chest, he realized he was also not breathing and attempted to unobtrusively draw much-needed air into his lungs.

Oh, Lord, his mind hammered, Hannah was a vision of loveliness. She was just so...so beautiful.

His gaze swept over her, missing no detail of her silky dark hair, those incredible big dark eyes, the white velvet texture of her skin. And her lips, those kissable lips, that were beckoning to him.

She was wearing a powder blue maternity dress with a gracefully draping bow tied at the neck and tiny pleats across the bodice. The slope of her stomach beneath the soft material was sensuously feminine. Her medium-heel navy blue pumps accentuated her shapely calves and slender ankles.

Hannah cocked her head slightly to one side, causing her hair to swing in an enticing dark curtain around her face. She looked at him questioningly.

"Ted?" she said. "Is something wrong?"

He blinked. "What? Oh!"

He stepped into the room and Hannah shut the door as he turned to face her, his heart thundering.

Then Hannah smiled.

"Oh, hell," he said, dropping his chin to his chest. He raised his head again and closed the distance between them. Framing her face in his hands, he lowered his head and kissed her.

Hannah's smothered gasp of surprise instantly changed into a purr of pleasure as she parted her lips to receive Ted's tongue. Her hands floated upward to encircle his neck as he wrapped his arms around her. The kiss deepened and passions soared.

It had been an eternity since he'd kissed Hannah, Ted thought hazily. A lifetime. Forever. He *needed* this kiss with an intensity beyond description. It was filling him with a warmth separate and apart from the heated desire coiling in his body.

Hannah, his mind hummed. *Yes.*

Hannah inched her fingertips into Ted's thick hair, urging his mouth harder onto hers, savoring his taste, aroma, the ecstasy of his tongue dueling with hers.

A part of her knew that kissing Ted was wrong. It was what she had pledged *not* to do ever again. But the other section of herself didn't care. The kiss was heavenly, and she wanted it to go on and on.

Ted lifted his head, drew a ragged breath, then shifted his hands to Hannah's shoulders, easing her away from his throbbing, aching body.

"Hannah," he said, then cleared his throat as he heard the gritty quality of his voice.

"Hmm?" she said dreamily, then ordered herself to pay attention to what Ted was saying. "Yes?"

"Don't go nuts because of that kiss. Okay? You know, don't whip your that-shouldn't-have-happened spiel on me, because it was a perfectly justifiable kiss."

"This ought to be good," she said, smiling. "All right, Ted, I'm all ears. Why was that a perfectly justifiable kiss?"

"Because, Ms. Doodle, it was a hello-Hannah-it's-good-to-see-you kiss. Neat and tidy. Get it?"

"You're so crazy." She laughed. "Okay, I won't go nuts. I'm glad to see you, too, Ted."

He matched her smile. "Well, good, that's great." He nodded. "Some things should be kept simple, uncomplicated. We wrapped that kiss in a nice little package and put a label on it. No problem."

"Whatever you say," she said, still smiling. "I can't always follow your out-of-left-field rationale, but I don't feel like arguing the point. I'll go get my purse and sweater.''

"Wait a minute," he said, not releasing her. "First of all, I want to tell you how pretty you look. You're really lovely, Hannah.''

"Oh, well, thank you. You look very spiffy yourself, Mr. Sharpe.''

"Subject two." His smile faded. "Did you give a concert of *Claire de Lune* to the entire building because you get a rush from playing *Claire de Lune* at sonic-level volume, or was it therapy because you're stressed about the evening ahead?''

Hannah sighed. "I admit I'm nervous. I suddenly didn't know why on earth I'd agreed to this outing. I would have canceled, but you seemed to have disappeared for the past few days.''

"I was around," he said. Man, he really was a clever son-of-a-gun. Creeping up the back stairs had been well worth the effort. "Look, there's nothing to be jittery about. You know me, and within ten minutes of meeting Deedee and Ryan, you'll feel as though you've known them for a long time. Trust me.''

He grimaced.

"Erase that. Bad choice of words. So, okay, don't dwell on whether or not to trust me. Just keep an open mind and be receptive. Yes? Yes. Let's go.''

Ted dropped his hands from her shoulders and glanced around the room.

"Hey, Daisy," he said. "There you are. Listen, kid, stay out of the refrigerator and don't watch any dirty flicks on the cable channels. Got that?''

Hannah laughed in delight at Ted's nonsense, then went to retrieve her purse and sweater.

As they left the apartment, she realized her jangled nerves were now calm, cool and collected, and she had a lovely sense of anticipation about the evening.

"Oh, my goodness," Hannah said. "I can't eat another bite. It was all so delicious, but I've definitely reached my limit."

"Waste not, want not," Ted said. He slid Hannah's plate in front of him and took a bite of the remainder of her cherry pie. "Mmm, not bad."

"When I was pregnant with Teddy," Deedee said, "I never seemed to fill up. I ate like a piggy the entire time. Jillian didn't have much of an appetite when she was carrying the triplets, though."

"She still ended up looking like a life raft," Ryan said.

Deedee rolled her eyes heavenward. "Don't you dare start *that* again. You're lucky you lived through your last crummy descriptions."

"Ah, yes," Hannah said, smiling. "I've been informed that I'm the size of a volleyball."

"You're hopeless, Ted," Deedee said.

"Why? Volleyballs are nice," he said, with a shrug. "I've never met a volleyball I didn't like. There's nothing insulting about being called a volleyball."

"We're ignoring you, Ted," Deedee said. "Hannah, have you started putting the baby's nursery together yet?"

"No, I need to explore the used-furniture stores. I'm hoping to find a crib, changing dresser, high chair, all of those sorts of things at reasonable prices."

"That's a good idea," Deedee said, nodding.

"Do those places deliver?" Ted said.

"Oh," Hannah said, frowning, "I didn't think about that."

"No problem," Ted said. "My Blazer can carry a lot in the back. We'll load it up and bring it all home."

He glanced up quickly at Hannah, Deedee and Ryan, all of whom were staring at him.

"To *your* home, Hannah," he said. "Your apartment, the place where Daisy allows you to live with her."

"Thank you, Ted," she said quietly. "That's a very generous offer, and I appreciate it. I realize you're busy, so I'll see if I can make a deposit on what I find, then we'll go get it."

"Not good," he said, pushing the now-empty plate to one side. "You might not know what to look for as far as construction, sturdiness, that sort of thing. I'd better tag along when you're shopping."

"I can't ask you to—"

"Take him with you," Ryan said. "It'll keep him off the streets and out of the bars. Listen, Ted, have a measuring tape with you to check the distance between the rungs on the crib. Some of the old ones aren't up to code."

Ted nodded. "Got it."

"Ask about lead-free paint, too," Ryan said. "That's very important."

"Let's leave the baby-furniture experts to their madness, Hannah," Deedee said. "You and I are off to the powder room."

"Why do they call it that?" Ted said. "I've never seen a woman trek in that direction with a big can of talcum powder."

Deedee got to her feet. "You are so strange, Ted Sharpe."

"Well, I think about stuff like that. Powder room. Lord, that's dumb."

Hannah laughed, then walked away with Deedee.

As Hannah and Deedee stood in front of the mirror in the powder room freshening their lipstick, Deedee suddenly laughed and shook her head.

"Darn that Ted," she said. "From now on, every time I go into a ladies' room, I'm going to be watching to see if anyone uses powder, even if it's only on their nose."

"I know what you mean," Hannah said, smiling. "I don't think Ted's mind ever stops." She paused, meeting Deedee's gaze in the reflection of the mirror. "Did you know that Ted bought me a darling kitten the day you got Teddy the puppy? Well, yes, I guess you were there when he found Daisy for me."

"No, actually, we had already headed for home with our bouncing beagle. Ted told us about Daisy later. He also shared the story of why you named her that. Your gran sounds like she was wonderful, Hannah."

"Yes. Yes, she was. And Daisy? She's so cute. She has really made my apartment seem more like a home, too. That probably doesn't make sense, but it's true. It was so thoughtful of Ted to get me a kitten."

"Ted Sharpe," Deedee said, nodding, "is a *very* nice man. You should see him with Teddy and the other MacAllister kids. He's a natural as a father. All the little guys absolutely adore him."

Hannah replaced the lipstick in her purse. "I can tell he's very fond of them, but he's made it clear that he's a Professional Uncle. That's in capital letters, I'll have you know. I'd say Ted is a confirmed bachelor."

"Oh, I don't know," Deedee said, snapping her purse closed. "Granted, he has industrial-strength sex appeal and women dissolve at his feet, but even the mighty tumble. He's just liable to go down for the count one of these days. You know, fall in love, get married, have a whole bushel of kids."

Hannah shrugged.

"Hannah Johnson," Deedee said, "that shrug spoke volumes. Don't you view Ted as an available man?"

"Well, yes, I suppose, but I'm not an available woman."

"Why not? Because you're expecting a baby?"

"There's that, plus the fact that I never intend to become seriously involved with a man again. Not ever."

"Oh, that's how you feel now," Deedee said breezily, while watching Hannah's face intently. "But we women are notorious for changing our minds."

"*I* won't. You see, Deedee, I lack the ability to determine whether a man is really who he presents himself to be. I have a track record of being very wrong."

Deedee smiled brightly. "But in Ted's case, you have reference letters, of a sort. I guarantee that he's really a good guy."

"No, he's a good *friend* to you and Ryan, and a super uncle to Teddy and the other MacAllister children. You have no way of really knowing how he treats women on a man-to-woman plane."

Deedee frowned. "Oh."

"And *I* don't intend to find out. Are you ready to go back to the table?"

"Wait, wait," Deedee said quickly. "You *are* going to allow Ted to be your friend, aren't you? Help you shop for baby furniture and what have you?"

"Well," Hannah said thoughtfully, "yes, I guess so. He *is* a good friend. Daisy is proof of that. Yes, I'd like Ted to be my friend." She walked toward the door.

"Well," Deedee mumbled, "that's a start."

The couples chatted comfortably over cups of coffee, then left the restaurant. In the parking lot, Deedee told Hannah she'd call soon so they could get together.

"Wonderful," Hannah said. "I'm eager to meet Teddy."

"And Scooter," Ryan said. "You just haven't experienced life until you've had Scooter MacAllister bounce straight up in the air and lick your nose. Man, that is one weird dog."

"Scooter is emotionally attached to Ryan's feet," Deedee said. "It's amazing."

"It's ridiculous," Ryan said.

"Scooter probably needs a dog shrink," Ted said. "You know, some guy to hold her paw and ask her how she got along with her mother."

"Oh, good grief," Hannah said, laughing.

Goodbyes were exchanged, and Ted was soon easing the Blazer out of the parking lot and into the busy traffic. He tuned the radio to an easy-listening station and soft, dreamy music filled the air.

A lovely sense of well-being floated over Hannah, causing a smile to form on her lips. With all the turmoil she'd endured in her life over the past months, she was acutely aware of how serene she felt, as though all was right with the world.

"Did you enjoy the evening?" Ted said.

"Oh, my, yes," she said. "It was lovely, absolutely perfect."

He nodded. "Good."

"I'm expressing my official thank-you, Ted, for tonight. I'll only say it once because you said I went nuts with all the thank-yous when you gave me Daisy. So... thank you."

"You're very welcome, Ms. Doodle. I had a great time myself and *I* thank *you* for that. I'm sure you could tell that Deedee and Ryan were more than pleased to meet and get to know you."

"They're marvelous." She paused. "No, the word you used was 'terrific,' and you were right. I'm so eager to see Teddy." She laughed. "And Scooter, the famous bouncing beagle."

"Okay, we'll make plans to go visit as soon as possible. We need to get shopping for baby furniture on the calendar, too."

"Yes."

We, we, we, Hannah's mind echoed. Ted said it so easily, so naturally, as though it was a given that they were a "we." It had a nice sound to it, made her feel warm inside.

There were times when the reality of her being alone caused a chill to sweep through her. It would sneak up on her when she least expected it, making the "alone" become "lonely."

We.

Such a small word, two letters, but it possessed remarkable powers for its size.

Tonight, just for tonight, she mused, she was going to keep and savor the soothing comfort of Ted's "we." The whole evening had been splendid, and she'd top it off with the warm fuzzy feeling his "we" evoked. There was no harm in indulging herself like this for a short time. It would be like having a snifter of rich brandy after a delicious meal.

With the dawn of tomorrow, she'd accept with a smile that her world comprised herself, the baby and Daisy. That was fine, the way it was. It would be a sunny daffodils-and-daisies day.

But tonight? Tonight, she was part of a "we."

At the apartment complex, Ted parked in his designated spot, then came around to assist Hannah from the vehicle. He encircled her shoulders with one arm, and she moved close to his side as they went into the building, then entered the elevator.

At her door, Ted extended his hand for her keys, which she placed in his palm.

"Coffee?" she said.

"Yes."

Daisy greeted them as Ted closed and locked the door behind them.

"Hi, Daisy," Hannah said, smiling. "Did you have a nice evening? Mine was marvelous."

"Yours," Ted said, "isn't quite over."

Hannah looked up at him and her breath caught as she saw the raw passion radiating from his blue eyes.

Oh, dear heaven, she thought frantically. There was no doubt whatsoever that Ted Sharpe wanted her, wanted to make love with her now, right now.

She had to move, run or shake his hand and say good-night. She had to do *something* to break the spell he was weaving over her with those mesmerizing eyes.

Ted lifted his hands and framed her face.

"We have to end this evening properly," he said, his voice low and husky. "We really do, Hannah."

We, her heart sang.

Ted lowered his head and captured her mouth.

And Hannah was lost in a sea of raging desire.

She parted her lips and met his tongue eagerly as her lashes drifted slowly down and her hands entwined his neck.

The kiss was ecstasy, heated and hungry, sensuous.

Sharpe, stop, Ted's mind hammered. He was losing control. He ached with the want of Hannah, was slipping past the point of reason, going right over the edge.

He tore his mouth from hers, forming the words *good night, Hannah* in his head, pulling them forward from the depths of the passion-laden haze that consumed him.

Say it, he mentally ordered himself. *Say, 'Good night, Hannah.'* "I want you, Hannah," he heard instead. "I want you so damn much."

Hannah opened her eyes slowly, and a soft, womanly smile formed on her moist lips.

"Yes," she whispered, "I know. I want you, too, Ted. We want each other, and it's right, it truly is, because... because it's *we.*"

Chapter Seven

A groan rumbled deep in Ted's chest as his mouth melted over Hannah's once again. He drank of her sweet taste, savoring it.

When he finally broke the kiss, she kept him close to her side as she led him down the hall to her bedroom. Hannah snapped on the small lamp on the nightstand, casting a rosy glow over the room, then brushed back the blankets on the bed. She straightened and looked at Ted.

Neither spoke, but words weren't needed.

It was as though they'd been transported to a magical world where thoughts were known, sent and received, understood.

There was an interwoven aura in the room of crackling sensuality, combined with the peaceful calmness of realizing that what they were about to share was so very right and real.

Ted drew Hannah into his arms and kissed her; gently, reverently, communicating the message that she was special, cherished.

She trembled.

He took a step backward and began to remove his clothes, dropping them unheeded to the floor. Hannah started to undress, placing the garments neatly on a chair by the nightstand.

Her back to Ted, Hannah suddenly stilled, her eyes skimming over her own naked body, seeing the heavy breasts, the protruding stomach where the baby was nestled. How would he view her swollen body? She reached out with a visibly shaking hand to retrieve her dress, to cover herself from Ted's scrutiny.

But Ted knew her thoughts as though she'd spoken aloud and he moved behind her and rested his hands on her shoulders. He dipped his head to bury his face in the silky cascade of her dark hair. Shifting his hands, he turned her toward him, slowly, so slowly, then looked directly into her eyes.

"Hannah," he said, "*we,* just like you said, *we* are the only ones in this world we're creating at this moment. Just the two of us."

"Yes," she whispered.

He smiled as he traced the shape of her lips with one fingertip, then dropped his gaze to her body, his smile changing to an expression of awe and wonder.

"Ah, Hannah," he said, his voice raspy. "You're so beautiful, so beautiful."

So beautiful, his mind echoed. She was woman personified. Femininity in its purest form. Within her was a miracle, a new life. She possessed the ability to nurture that baby, carry it safely until it was ready to meet the world. It was breathtaking. Wondrous.

Ted lifted one hand, then tentatively splayed it across her rounded stomach.

He met her gaze again and Hannah smiled at him warmly, her flicker of fear now forgotten.

She felt...beautiful, she realized, so incredibly feminine. She was woman. And Ted was the epitome of man. It was so simplistic, yet held the complexity of a wonderful mystery never to be solved.

Her eyes roamed boldly over his naked body, savoring the sight of his broad shoulders and chest, his flat belly and powerful legs, his arousal that announced his want of her, the blatant desire that *she* had evoked.

She inched her fingertips into the moist curls on his chest, relishing the feel of them and the taut muscles beneath.

Ted leaned toward her to kiss her and she parted her lips to receive his questing tongue. Moments later, he ended the kiss, lifted her into his arms, then laid her gently in the center of the bed. He stretched out next to her, resting on one forearm.

"You're exquisite," he said, his voice rough with passion. "I want you, Hannah, but it's more than that. This..." His gaze swept over her, then back to her eyes. "This is a miracle you're sharing with me, and I'm honored, I truly am."

"Oh, Ted," she said, unexpected tears misting her eyes. "What a lovely thing to say. Thank you."

"No, *I'm* thanking *you.*"

They touched, caressed, explored. Lips followed where hands had gone, glorying in each new discovery. Passions soared until their breathing was labored and hearts beat wildly.

Finally, *finally,* Ted moved over her, keeping his weight from her on straightened arms as he entered her. He watched her face for any sign that he was hurting her, but saw only want and need as raw and earthy as his own.

"Yes," Hannah whispered. "Oh, Ted, yes."

He started to move, slowly at first, then with increasing tempo. She matched him, meeting him, welcoming him, as she clutched his shoulders.

Tension began to build within them tighter, hotter, coiling in spiraling currents. Lifting them up and away from reality.

Higher.

Soaring.

"Ted!"

Hannah was flung far, far beyond anything she had ever known before to a wondrous place of sparkling colors and intense physical sensations that defied description.

Ted joined her there a heartbeat later. Throwing back his head, a groan of pure male pleasure rumbled from his throat as he found his release.

They stilled, hovering for a second, for eternity. Memorizing the moment, etching it indelibly in their hearts and minds; their very souls.

Then Ted shifted off of Hannah and collapsed next to her, spent, sated, staying close to her side.

And neither spoke, because no words were needed.

Ted reached for the blankets and covered them as their bodies cooled. He kissed Hannah on the temple, then snapped off the lamp.

"Go to sleep, Ms. Doodle," he said quietly.

"Yes," she said, snuggling closer to him.

As Hannah drifted into blissful slumber, Ted placed one hand on her stomach in a protective gesture. He looked at Hannah's peaceful face again, then back at his hand.

A strange tightness gripped his throat and his eyes burned with what he realized were unshed tears. Emotions tumbled through him in a maze, too many and too foreign to decipher.

He closed his eyes, took a deep, ragged breath, then gave way to the somnolence that claimed him.

Ted was pulled from the depths of a deep, peaceful and dreamless sleep by a strange, irritating sensation. Even in his foggy state, he realized there was something moist stroking his chin in a steady rhythm.

He opened one eye and saw Daisy curled next to him on the pillow, her full attention devoted to giving his chin a morning bath.

Ted frowned in confusion, wondering how Daisy had gotten into his apartment. In the next instant, reality struck and he snapped his head around to look at the pillow next to him. The jerking motion caused Daisy to tumble away in a fluffy ball, complete with an indignant squeak of protest.

Hannah, Ted thought, staring at her. Beautiful Ms. Doodle. She slept pretty. Yeah, she really did. Her hair was spread out on the pillow like a dark, silky fan, her features were relaxed and lovely, her lips...those sensational, kissable, sweet-as-honey lips, were slightly parted. A cameo.

The events of the previous night floated into Ted's mental vision, vivid and sensuously detailed. Heat came to life in his body, causing the now-familiar ache of wanting Hannah to build steadily. He tore his gaze from her face to look beyond her to the clock on the nightstand.

It read 7:12 a.m.

It was a new day, Sunday morning, he mused. What would Hannah do, say? How would she feel about having made love with him? Would this be, to her, a daffodils-and-daisies morning? Or would she be filled with regret, remorse? Demand that he leave her bed, her home, her life?

Lord, what if she said he was never to darken her doorway again? Tossed him out and slammed the door, locking it firmly behind him?

Well, there was no way to know what her frame of mind, her mood or attitude was until she woke up. He'd just stay put and wait patiently for her to open her big, gorgeous dark eyes.

Ted stared at the ceiling for two seconds, three, then four.

"Hell, forget it," he mumbled.

He raised his head to see Daisy sitting by his knee, busily grooming her tail. He scooped up the kitten and placed her gently on the pillow next to Hannah's face.

"Go for it, Daisy," he whispered.

Rolling onto his side, he propped himself up on one forearm, then nudged Daisy on the bottom. The kitten inched forward, leaned toward Hannah, studied the sleeping human, then began to wash Hannah's nose.

Ted smothered a chuckle before it could erupt.

Hannah frowned in her sleep, then brushed a hand in the direction of the annoying whatever-it-was on her nose, missing Daisy entirely. The busy little pink tongue continued its chore.

"Mmm," Hannah said, opening her eyes, which immediately crossed as she focused on Daisy. "Oh, good grief, would you go away?"

"Good morning," Ted said quietly.

Hannah's eyes flew to his, then widened for a moment at the shock of seeing him there.

Ted's heart thudded wildly as he met her gaze. He willed her to speak, to give him some clue as to what she was feeling, before he had a nervous breakdown.

He did *not* want Hannah to regret what they'd shared. Why that was so very important to him, he had no idea, but it was. And if she didn't say something in the next second, he was going to go right out of his ever-lovin' mind.

"Hannah," he said, hearing the unsteady tone of his voice, "it's a daffodils-and-daisies morning." He paused and lifted Daisy off the pillow, putting her farther down the bed between him and Hannah. "Right?"

Hannah continued to stare at him, no readable expression on her face. A trickle of sweat ran down Ted's chest as he waited, hardly breathing.

Then slowly, so slowly, a smile began to form on Hannah's lips.

"Yes, Ted," she said softly. "It *is* a daffodils-and-daisies morning."

Ted flopped back onto his pillow. "Oh, thank God." He dragged both hands down his face, then turned his head to look at her again. "I was so afraid that you'd... Never mind."

"That I'd be sorry about what happened last night? Be filled with guilt or regret?"

"Well, yeah. I mean, I know that you wouldn't treat something like this lightly. Believe me, Hannah, I *do* know that. I'd hate it, really hate it, if you were upset, angry, sorry it took place, whatever. But...you're not?"

"No."

"Why not?"

"Isn't just saying no enough?" she said, frowning slightly.

"Humor me. I'm a wreck here, Hannah. I've been waiting hours for you to wake up so I'd know how you felt about this. Well, that's stretching it a bit. It wasn't hours, but it sure seemed like it was. I'm shook up here, Ms. Doodle, so take pity and tell me why this is a daffodils-and-daisies day."

"Well, because we made exquisite love together, Ted," she said, her smile returning. "It was glorious, like nothing I've ever experienced before. You made me feel special, cherished, and…and beautiful. Even though I'm shaped like a volleyball, I felt beautiful.''

Heat rocketed through Ted's body as he listened to Hannah's softly spoken words and saw the gentle, womanly smile on her face.

Ah, Hannah, his mind thundered. *I want you again. Now. Right now.*

''And,'' she went on, ''I'm a woman who is free to make her own decisions as long as I realize I have to take responsibility for them. I wanted to make love with you, Ted. So I made the choice to do so, and I'm not sorry that I did. There. That's it. Last night was last night. Today is a new day. End of story.''

Ted frowned. ''Wait a minute. That doesn't sound quite right to me.''

''What's wrong with it?''

''Last night isn't erased, forgotten or wrapped up in a package and shoved onto a back shelf somewhere. It has a bearing on this morning. It came with us into the new day. You can't separate the two like cutting a pizza.''

''Yes, I can, and I have.'' She paused. ''Would you like some breakfast? I make a delicious omelet, if I do say so myself.''

''Hold it,'' he said, slicing one hand through the air. He sat up, shoved the pillow against the headboard, then moved backward to lean against it. The sheet and blanket dropped, then draped low across his hips. ''We haven't finished this discussion yet.''

Hannah clutched the sheet over her bare breasts with one hand, then wiggled into a position matching Ted's.

Daisy yowled her disapproval at being disturbed and jumped off the bed, rolling head over tail when she landed on the floor. She shook herself, then ran from the room.

Hannah tucked the sheet beneath her arms, then folded her hands on her stomach. She looked at Ted and raised her eyebrows.

"What?" he said, obviously confused.

"You called this meeting to order," she said. "Go ahead and speak your mind. Do be aware, however, that I'm eating for two, and this duo is hungry. Well? Carry on, Mr. Sharpe."

"I most certainly will. You, Ms. Doodle, have a wacky attitude, do you know that? You put things into slots, compartments, or something, then close the door, lock it and ignore them."

Hannah nodded thoughtfully. "You're right...sort of. I mean, you're basically correct, but the way you describe it makes it sound as though I do it on a whim, like I'm just shrugging and saying, 'Oh, well, what the hell.'"

"Mmm," he said, crossing his arms firmly over his chest. "Mmm."

"You're starting to get angry, and that's not fair, Ted. I don't have an 'attitude' in the negative way you said it. I have a philosophy for living my life, one that has made it possible for me to survive some rough blows. If I get mired in the past, it would be impossible to be in the now, then move forward into the future."

"That's fine, dandy, really great. I can see where that philosophy helped you deal with the reality of your husband being a total jerk. But Hannah, we made love last night. A handful of hours ago. I think it's lousy that you've put it away somewhere like yesterday's newspaper. Damn it, what we shared was important!''

"Don't yell! I know it was important, and special and... But, darn it, don't you see that if I bring it into today, I'm giving it the power to dictate to my emotions, my state of mind?

"What do you want me to do? Go around with a silly grin on my face, staring dreamily into space and sighing as I say 'Ted, oh, Ted. Oh, Ted, Ted, Ted,' like a besotted teenager?''

Ted narrowed his eyes. "That has possibilities. It's a helluva lot better than my feeling like old news, like I'm Mr. 'What's-his-name.' ''

"Ah-ha," she said, pointing one finger in the air. "Oops," she said as the sheet began to slip down. She tucked it back into place.

"Ah-ha? That indicates you've drawn some sort of conclusion. Do enlighten me, Hannah. I'd hate to miss this.''

"It's as clear as a bell. Your male ego is bruised, Mr. Sharpe." She nodded decisively. "You're accustomed to women being all dewy-eyed and breathless the morning after. Despite the fact that you're a confirmed bachelor who wants no part of commitment or entanglements, you don't know what to do with a woman who cherishes having made love with you last night, but greets the morning thinking of omelets.''

"Oh, man," he said, squeezing his temples with one hand. "You're scrambling my brain. I've never met anyone like you before, anyone who thinks like you do. You are definitely driving me crazy.''

''I don't know why, because it's very simple. Well, maybe it's complicated to you, but it's simple in its complexity.'' She laughed. ''That didn't make one bit of sense.''

''No joke. I need some time to sort through this puzzle. That means I'm not yet in a position to convince you to allow last night to be part of today.

''However, since I feel so strongly that our lovemaking should be in the here and now, I'll have to make adjustments to the situation until I have a clearer picture of this maze.''

''What sort of adjustments?''

''Elementary, my dear Doodle. It's called compromise. We'll leave what we shared in last night's slot, where you feel it belongs, even though I adamantly disagree.

''So, in order to keep our making love in today, where I believe it deserves to be, we'll take care of today's slot, which you decree to be empty. Get it?''

''Oh. Well, yes, I do understand what you're saying, but...''

''Lord, I'm brilliant.'' He slid one hand to the back of her neck and leaned toward her. ''I amaze myself at times with my genius-level thinking.''

''But...''

He brushed his lips over hers. ''Don't you agree, Hannah—'' he traced her lips with the tip of his tongue ''—that I'm extremely intelligent?''

''I...um...''

Ted slipped the sheet free of her arms and swept it away, his hand returning to tenderly cradle one of her breasts.

"Yes?" he said, close to her lips.

"Yes," she said breathlessly. "Oh, yes."

It was all, and it was more, than the exquisite love-making of the night before. It was slow, teasing, tantalizing. Hands and lips were never still; roaming, caressing with feather-like gentleness, discovering more of the mysteries freely revealed.

"Ah, Hannah," Ted said, his voice hoarse with building passion.

He kissed her stomach, then his breath caught as he felt the baby move. He splayed one hand on the rounded flesh, awe evident on his face and in his eyes as the miracle beneath shifted again.

"Incredible," he whispered. "My God, Hannah, do you realize what you're sharing with me? What you're allowing me to be a part of? Thank you. Oh, Hannah, thank you. I sincerely mean that."

He captured her mouth and kissed her deeply, foreign emotions intertwining with his raging desire.

Ted, Ted, Ted, Hannah's mind sang. Besotted teenager? Oh, who cared? It didn't matter, not now. She'd think later . . . later. She just wanted Ted, needed Ted, before she went up in flames and disappeared into oblivion.

He entered her slowly, his arms trembling from forced restraint. She met his smoldering gaze, knowing desire showed in her eyes, as well.

"Please," she said, pressing her hands more firmly on his back. "Come to me, Ted. I want you so much, so very much."

He thrust deeper, and a sigh of pleasure escaped from Hannah's lips.

"Oh, Ted," she said dreamily.

He stilled within her, savoring the moist heat that had received all he'd brought to her, welcoming him into the dark, feminine haven of her body.

"This is today, Hannah," he said, the raspy quality of his voice sounding strange to his own ears. "We're making love *today*."

"A daffodils-and-daisies day."

"Yes."

He kissed her again, then began a rocking rhythm. Hannah moved with him in perfect synchronization. He increased the tempo and they began to soar, each anticipating the summit; wishing to postpone it, yet wanting, needing it, now.

They reached the pinnacle seconds apart, each calling the name of the other, holding on tightly.

They were there . . . and it was glorious.

It was a celebration of man being man, woman being woman, counterparts meant to mesh into one entity that was creating an ecstasy far beyond definition in its splendor.

They drifted among the spectacle of vibrant, sparkling colors, delaying the return, staying in a world that belonged only to them.

Reality tapped gently on hazy minds, and Ted reluctantly moved from Hannah to settle close to her side.

"Oh, Ted," she said. "Oh, my goodness."

"Ditto, kiddo," he said, then drew a deep, steadying breath. "Unreal. I'll move in a week. Just dust around me."

Hannah smiled. "Okay. However, as unromantic as this statement is about to be, my human cargo just plunked himself, or herself, on my bladder. As the saying goes, 'I'm outta here.'" She kissed Ted quickly on the lips, then left the bed, hurrying to the bathroom.

Ted closed his eyes, savoring the sated contentment consuming him.

Hannah, his mind hummed.

He opened his eyes, laced his fingers beneath his head and stared up at the ceiling. A frown crept over his features.

Hannah was so different from any woman he'd ever known. She was evoking emotions within him that he couldn't clearly identify.

Was he headed for trouble?

Was he being drawn deeper and deeper into a situation where he didn't belong?

Should he exit stage left immediately?

No!

Damn it, no.

He was okay, doing fine. Of course he felt a protectiveness toward Hannah, any decent man would, considering her circumstances. As for the foreign emotions, he'd ignore them. What he didn't address couldn't affect him. That made sense.

He was still determined to convince Hannah that her resolve to never love again was wrong. There was no reason for her to sentence herself to a life alone, just her and the baby.

The baby. Lord, when he'd felt the baby move, he thought his heart was going to jump right out of his chest. Beneath his lips, his hand, a miracle had made its presence known. Incredible. Awesome. Humbling.

"Really something," he said aloud.

So, Sharpe? he asked himself. *Have you got your act together?* Yeah, he did. Making love with Hannah didn't mean he'd *fall in love* with Ms. Doodle. No way.

But he'd stick close to her, help her fix up the nursery, show her, prove to her over time that he was exactly who he said he was. Not *all* men changed their stripes after gaining a woman's trust.

Once she realized that *he* was real, she'd have to admit that there must be other guys out there who were, too. Then she'd...

Ted sat bolt upward.

Then she'd what? Fall in love with one of *them?* Make love with one of *them?* Pick one of *them* to have the privilege of helping her raise her child?

Well, yeah, that was the ultimate goal of his campaign.

So why did he suddenly have a cold knot in his gut?

"Because you're hungry, fool," he said, flipping back the blankets.

He needed some protein, some brain food, then he'd be right as rain. Everything would be fine, under his control.

Chapter Eight

That evening, Ted dropped a sponge into a plastic pail filled with soapy water, then stepped back and planted his hands on his hips.

"There you go, Ms. Doodle," he said. "Crib, high chair, playpen and changing table are assembled and washed with soap and disinfectant. I'd say we've done a good day's work."

"*You* did all the work," Hannah said, smiling. "I just stood around watching."

"Every job needs a supervisor. This stuff is in excellent condition, considering it's used. I think it looks great."

"Oh, it does." Hannah swept her gaze over the room. "It's a nursery. This morning it was an empty room, and now it's an honest-to-goodness nursery."

"Yup."

"It makes the baby seem even more real. I guess that sounds dumb, but I look at that crib and I can visualize a little one sleeping there." She laughed. "I'm going to have a baby."

Ted chuckled. "Yes, ma'am. You certainly are, ma'am." He paused and frowned. "The drawers in the changing table sure are empty. I guess next up is to start getting those sleeper gizmos, diapers, blankets, bibs, the whole nine yards."

"Yes. There's a place called Grandma's House that sells used baby and children's clothes. I'm going to see what they have."

Ted picked up the pail and started toward the bedroom door.

"Ted?"

He stopped, then half turned to look back at her. "Hmm?"

"Thank you so much for all you did today. I can't begin to tell you how much I appreciate it."

"You just told me. Come on, I'm a starving man. I've got a couple of pizzas in the freezer. Let's go to my place and stick them in the oven."

"You can't feed me dinner on top of everything else you've done for me today."

"Sure I can. I'm in the mood for some cheap, cardboard pizza. I'll dump this water, then we're on our way."

In Ted's apartment, Hannah made a quick scrutiny of the living room.

"Your apartment is the reverse of mine. Everything goes in the opposite direction." She smiled. "I'd better stay alert or I'm liable to walk into a wall."

"Another big difference is that your place is neat as a pin. I'm a slob, pure and simple."

"What do you use your second bedroom for? A guest room? Office? Nothing?"

"Take a look if you want to," he said. "I'll go put the pizzas in the oven."

When Ted entered the spare bedroom ten minutes later, he found Hannah peering into the glass-fronted cabinet. She turned to face him, her dark eyes sparkling.

"Oh, Ted, these miniatures are beautiful. I had no idea you were so talented."

"Well, that's stretching it a bit. They come in kits. I have to carve away the excess, but it's not as if I start from scratch with a hunk of wood. I enjoy it, though. It's very relaxing."

"That tiny cradle you're doing now is exquisite. The details are incredible for something so small. I'm standing firm on my statement that you're very talented."

"Whatever. Next I'm going to build a dollhouse to hold all this stuff. I bought a book at Deedee's store and I have to decide which one to make."

"Could I see the book?"

"Sure. Bring it out to the table. I need to check on the pizzas. Cardboard doesn't take long to cook."

"I'll help with dinner," she said. "Do you want me to set the table, or pour the drinks?"

"Nope. You've been on your feet a lot today. It's time you put your bottom on a chair."

Hannah laughed. "Says the expert on such things?"

"Hey, I hang out with the MacAllister clan, remember? I've heard, 'Put your feet up, drink your milk, here's a pillow for behind your back,' and a long list of other things during the pregnancies I've witnessed. I'm very good at the waiting-room-at-the-hospital bit, too."

He handed her the book on making dollhouses and they left the room.

"However," he said, circling Hannah's shoulders with his arm, "if you want to know if you're having a girl or a boy, you'll have to ask Forrest MacAllister. He's The Baby Bet champion. The guy never misses. It's really getting creepy."

"Forrest *always* wins The Baby Bet?"

"Yup, and some of them have been very high-tech bets. When Forrest said Jillian was going to have triplets and they'd all be girls, I figured he was cooked. But I'll be damned if Jillian didn't have three baby girls. When you meet Forrest, just ignore the gleam he'll get in his eyes. He'll look at your volleyball and start mentally counting twenty-dollar bills."

"Oh, I doubt that I'd have occasion to meet Forrest MacAllister."

Ted stopped, forcing Hannah to do the same. He dropped his arm and moved to stand in front of her, placing both hands on her shoulders.

"Of course you'll be meeting Forrest...and Jillian, the kids, Jenny and Michael and...well, the whole gang." He frowned. "You want to, don't you?

They're all as nice as Ryan and Deedee, and you liked *them*."

"Yes, I did like them very much, but—"

"Listen, the MacAllisters get together all the time and I'm included in whatever they do. There's no reason why you can't go with me to birthday parties, potlucks, that kind of thing. It'll be fun, and you can talk about babies with the other moms to your heart's content."

"But what about the...the women you date? I mean, won't someone, or someones, get upset if you take *me* to where you've always taken them?"

"No, Ms. Doodle, because I've never taken a woman to a MacAllister gathering. The women I date aren't the type who would enjoy those sorts of outings. *You* will enjoy them, so you'll go with me. Okay?"

"But—"

"Hey, would you deprive Forrest of the opportunity to anticipate The Baby Bet being put into operation down the line? That would *not* be nice. The guy gets a major rush from The Baby Bet, along with a big stack of twenty-dollar bills."

"I—"

"Oh, hell, my cardboard pizzas are burning!"

The pizzas were very well done around the edges, but eatable. Ted placed a glass of soda by Hannah's plate, then produced a glass of milk, which he set next to the soft drink.

"Soda with a milk chaser?" she said, raising her eyebrows.

"Mothers-to-be need their milk," he said, sitting down opposite her. "I know about this jazz, remember?"

"If I drink two full glasses like those, I'll float away."

"Okay, then skip the soda and go for the milk."

"Pizza and milk? Yuck."

"Tough. There's a cow somewhere who donated that to your cause. The least you can do is drink it to show your gratitude for its contribution."

Hannah laughed.

"Hey, wait." Ted got to his feet, went into the kitchen and returned with a bowl of green grapes. "There you go." He plunked the bowl in front of Hannah.

"Pizza, milk and grapes?" she said. "This combination is getting worse by the minute."

"Fresh fruit is good for you. We may be starting a whole new eating fad with that menu you have there. We'll sell the idea to a fast-food chain and make a bundle." He leaned toward her. "Eat."

"Mmm," she said, glaring at him.

To Hannah's surprise, having pizza, milk and grapes together wasn't all that bad, a fact she decided not to share with the smug Mr. Sharpe.

"Ted," she said a few minutes later, "why are you so determined that I mix and mingle with the Mac-Allister family? I *do* have friends, you know. I'm not some pathetic orphaned waif who's all alone in the big, cruel world."

Ted frowned. "I realize that, but you did mention that your teacher friends don't have kids. People with

see is what you get, upfront and honest. If I'm being nice to you, it's because you're a nice person who deserves to be treated nicely. That's an overdose of the word *nice,* but that's how it is. Pure and simple."

"Oh," Hannah said, nodding. "Oh-h-h," she wailed in the next instant as tears filled her eyes. "I can't handle this."

"Jeez." Ted pulled the bowl of grapes toward him. "Quit eating these things."

Hannah sniffled. "I'm sorry. I just... But I... So sorry..." She threw up her hands in a gesture of frustration. "Oh-h-h."

Ted got to his feet. "You're exhausted, that's what you are. We did a lot today, too much, obviously. Come on, sweet Hannah, I'll walk you home so you can go to bed. Get some sleep and...bingo... tomorrow will be a daffodils-and-daisies day. Guaranteed."

Hannah nodded, sniffled again, then got to her feet. She welcomed the feel of Ted's powerful body as he slid one arm across her shoulders and tucked her close to his side.

She was suddenly so tired that it was an effort to place one foot in front of the other, and she was most definitely too exhausted to think. She would allow herself the luxury of being taken care of for now; escorted to her door, told to go to bed. So be it.

At Hannah's apartment, Ted unlocked the door, pushed it open and gave her the keys. Then he cradled her face in his hands and kissed her deeply.

"Sleep well, Ms. Doodle," he said when he finally raised his head.

"Thank you, Ted," she said, tears still echoing in her voice, "for everything."

Ted chuckled. "Especially that gourmet dinner I fixed you." He brushed his lips over hers. "Go."

Ted waited until he heard the lock snap into place and the jingle of the safety chain. He stared at the closed door for a long moment, then turned and walked slowly back to his own place.

In his living room, he stopped and gazed at his surroundings, seeing Hannah in his mind's eye, hearing her voice, her laughter, inhaling the lingering fragrance of flowers.

He crossed the room to the cluttered table and picked up the glasses, smiling as he looked at the bowl of green grapes.

He should be ticked, he supposed, at the way Hannah had switched moods and geared up for battle. But he couldn't be angry because she'd been so endearing, so befuddled by his actions. And he understood that she'd verbally attacked him because she'd been so badly hurt in the past.

And then she'd lost it, burst into tears and looked so tired and forlorn. He wanted to scoop her up and hold her, comfort her, tell her there was nothing to be afraid of when she was with him.

Ted took the glasses to the kitchen, then returned to the table to retrieve more of the debris. A frown settled over his features as he continued his cleaning chore.

Hannah's theory of how she was handling the issue of their lovemaking was unusual, to say the least. She placed it in its ever-famous slot and left it there.

Weird.

Well, maybe not. The women he slept with did the same thing, in their own way. They didn't expect anything of him the next day, just said, "see ya," and were receptive when he contacted them for another date.

So why did it bother him so much that Hannah insisted on leaving in the bedroom the intimacy they shared, refusing to allow it to have any influence whatsoever on the other hours they spent together?

Her attitude wasn't all that different from what he was accustomed to, what he actually preferred. So why had he been on her case, insisting her outlook was completely nuts? he wondered.

Hell, he didn't know.

He'd felt a knot tighten in his gut when Hannah had cut loose with her tirade, demanding to know why he wanted to take her to MacAllister events. That knot had been fear that she'd refuse to go. He wanted to have her with him when he took part in things with the MacAllister clan, he really did.

Sharpe, he told himself, *you'd better watch your step.* Hannah Johnson was getting to him, inch by emotional inch. He had to stay very alert, be certain he didn't get caught up by Hannah's bleak circumstances, continually see himself as the dashing hero to the rescue, her knight in shining armor arriving to save the damsel in distress.

What he'd told her was the truth. He enjoyed her company, and sincerely believed she'd reap great rewards from associating with the MacAllisters, from having them as friends.

And what she would learn over time was that there really were nice men around, the real goods. She'd see that a few mistakes in judgment in the past shouldn't sentence her to a life alone.

Yup, he thought, sticking the bowl of grapes into the refrigerator, everything would be just fine.

Ted wandered back into the living room. Then why was he so hell-bent on changing Hannah's attitude about keeping their lovemaking separate. Why did the idea of having Hannah by his side at the next Mac-Allister gathering hold so much appeal?

And why did it suddenly seem so damn quiet and empty in his living room?

"Forget it," he said aloud. "Go carve a cradle."

On his way to the spare bedroom, Ted changed directions and went to the table to retrieve the book on making dollhouses.

As he started back across the room, he flipped through the pages.

He'd pick the model that struck his fancy, he thought, and send for the kit. It would be a challenging and complicated project, but he'd enjoy it. Besides, he needed a house for his growing collection of furniture.

After turning on the light in the bedroom-workshop, Ted leaned one shoulder against the door frame and his gaze roamed over the room.

This was not, he supposed, remotely close to what people would expect to find in a so-called swinging bachelor's apartment. Fast-lane guys were not known for having a collection of handmade miniatures in residence, or for being in the process of deciding which dollhouse to build for the tiny furniture.

He frowned and shook his head.

It was actually borderline dumb, now that he really thought about it. A single man was intending to eventually have a completely furnished dollhouse in the spare bedroom of his apartment? *Definitely* dumb.

So, yeah, the MacAllister kids could visit it and play with it, but still.... A dollhouse belonged in a little girl's room where she could give free rein to her imagination whenever the mood struck. A dollhouse was something a daddy could share with her, too. They'd sit on the floor together, rearrange the furniture, make up stories about the people who lived in the house. Very special memories could be created by the hours a man spent with his daughter and a dollhouse.

Ted sighed.

A daughter. A miracle. A living, breathing human being, who existed because two people had joined their bodies in the most intimate and beautiful act ever.

A daughter or a son, neither of which he would ever have.

A chill coursed through Ted and he pushed himself away from the door frame and went to the chair by the worktable. He sank onto it heavily, placing the dollhouse book in front of him.

His mind was yanked back in time, haunting ghosts of the past giving no quarter. Over the years, he'd not allowed the truth the space to tear him apart, he'd refused to address what he knew was true.

But tonight? He was suddenly powerless against the memories that assaulted him....

He was sixteen years old and had just recovered from a severe case of the mumps. The doctor had run a test to see if any permanent damage had been done, and he and his parents were waiting for the results.

It was raining, and had been a gloomy day, ominously dark when it should have been sunny. He'd approached the kitchen door, then stopped in the hallway as he heard his parents talking.

"That was the doctor on the phone, Maggie," his father said. "Ted's test results show that he... Oh, God."

"Dean?" his mother said. "Dear heaven, what did the doctor say?"

"Ted... Ted is sterile because of his having had the mumps. He'll never father a child. Dear Lord, do you realize what he's been robbed of, what this means?"

Ted had turned, run down the hall, and barreled out the front door into the cold rain. He'd run as fast and far as he could before sinking to his knees in an empty field, his lungs burning.

He knew what his father had been about to say and hadn't been able to bear hearing it.

He'd been robbed of his manhood.

He was not, nor would he ever be, a whole man.

Ted had sprawled facedown on the wet grass, sobbing, his tears mingling with the driving rain that pelted him, his father's words echoing over and over in his mind, tormenting him.

From that day forward, there had been something missing from his relationship with his father, a breach that had never been repaired. He knew that in his father's eyes he now fell short of what a son should be.

Robbed of his manhood.

Not a whole man.

Ted had listened when his parents told him gently about the test results. He'd shrugged, said it was no big deal, and it had never been discussed again.

His folks never knew about the tears he'd shed, the pain he'd buried deep within himself.

The years had passed, he'd become a police officer, and lived the life of a swinging single. For weeks, months at a stretch, he was actually convinced that his existence was exactly the way he wanted it.

Then the ghosts would rear their ugly heads in the dark hours and he'd struggle against them. Push them away, winning each battle before they could grip his heart and soul.

Always winning . . . until tonight.

A shudder ripped through him and Ted dragged his hands down his face, his fingers trembling as he realized they were wet with tears.

"Oh, damn," he said, staring up at the ceiling.

He leaned forward, propped his elbows heavily on the table and sank his head into his hands. Time lost meaning as he sat there, alone and cold, empty, wrapped in a cocoon of misery.

Hannah lay in bed, willing sleep to come and carry her off into blissful oblivion. The baby was especially active tonight, probably objecting to the dinner menu of pizza and green grapes.

She turned her head toward the other pillow she couldn't see in the dark, envisioning how magnificent

Ted had looked there, close, his attention centered on her and the world they'd created together.

Daisy crawled up the bedspread, then settled by Hannah's waist and went to sleep. Hannah stroked the kitten absently, deep in thought.

Her ridiculous performance at Ted's had been just that...ridiculous. She'd been smiling one moment, picking a fight in the next breath, then had trekked right into being a weepy mess. How mortifying. How patient and sweet Ted had been.

Maybe she should blame the whole episode on pregnancy hormones and green grapes, and forget it.

Hannah sighed.

She'd never get away with a cop-out like that, because she knew it wasn't true. Ted was throwing her off-kilter, confusing her, making her nervous.

Because he was being just so darn nice.

She'd fallen prey to his damnable *niceness* throughout the day, had relaxed and enjoyed their shopping spree for the baby furniture.

Ted's enthusiasm had been infectious, and she'd felt happy and carefree. She'd laughed in pure delight when he whipped out his tape measure to check the crib slats, as Ryan had instructed. He'd been so serious about it, insisting on measuring every one, refusing to assume that if the first few met code, the rest would.

As she'd watched him, she made no attempt to hide the smile that remained on her face, and had been aware of a lovely warmth filling her, stroking her like a comforting blanket she could gather around herself.

Ted obviously objected to her plan to keep their lovemaking in its proper place. Why? He should be pleased and relieved that she didn't view their intimacy as a right to demand some sort of commitment from him.

Oh, he was a complicated man, so difficult to understand at times, so honest and open at others. He was weaving his way into her life, her day-to-day existence, and that was very dangerous.

Should she refuse to see him again?

Decline invitations to accompany him to MacAllister outings?

Not allow herself to share in exquisitely beautiful lovemaking with him ever again?

"Oh, dear," she whispered into the darkness.

That all sounded so bleak, so lonely. Ted made her smile, laugh right out loud. And Ted made her feel beautiful.

She didn't want to force him out of her life, not now, not yet.

Hannah frowned as a new thought struck her.

She wouldn't have to send Ted on his way later. He'd leave on his own, hightail it out of her life in the very near future.

Why?

Because she was pregnant. He might think her volleyball stomach was intriguing, but she was going to be much bigger than a *volleyball* before this baby was born.

She'd be fat, pure and simple. She'd waddle like a duck, forget what her feet looked like, be as attractive as a blimp. She might even grow to life-raft size, as Jillian had.

Hannah told herself she wouldn't have to work at not becoming too emotionally involved with Ted Sharpe because he wouldn't be around that long. Nature would take care of the job for her as the baby grew. She'd prepare herself for his inevitable exit stage left, and enjoy his company in the meantime.

After all, Ted was a confirmed bachelor who existed in the fast lane of the singles' scene because that was the life-style he preferred and intended to keep.

When she began to impersonate a whale, he'd be gone by *his* choice, *his* decision.

The only thing *she* had to do was make certain when Ted left, he didn't take her heart with him.

Chapter Nine

The following weeks passed quickly, one flowing into the next. Hannah and Ted were together at some point each day, depending on his shift. They shopped for baby clothes, attended MacAllister clan events, and spent a great many quiet and lovely evenings at home.

"Ted?" Hannah said.

"Hmm?"

"Would you put the VCR on stop, please? I need to talk to you about something."

Ted snapped his head around to look at Hannah where she sat next to him on the sofa in his living room.

"Sure," he said.

He pressed a button on the remote control and the

movie they had been watching halted just as the sheriff reached for his gun to shoot the outlaw.

"You're frowning," he said, matching her expression. "What's wrong?"

"Nothing. I mean, well, it's not nothing exactly, it's..." She took a steadying breath. "I went to the doctor today for my routine checkup."

Ted shifted on the sofa to fully face her. "And? What did he say? Why are you frowning? You were very quiet during dinner, preoccupied. Hannah? Talk to me," he said anxiously.

"I *am* talking to you, but you're taking up the air space."

"Oh. Sorry. Go ahead. You went to the doctor today. And?" He leaned toward her.

"This is November first, the beginning of my eighth month."

"And?"

"Well, he said that...um..."

"Hannah, please," Ted said, taking her hands in his. "Is the baby all right?"

"Oh, yes, he's fine. She's fine. Maybe I should have had an ultrasound. This 'he' or 'she' gets to be a nuisance sometimes."

"Forrest is gearing up to let you know what it is. We're getting closer to The Baby Bet extravaganza. Hannah, please, take pity on me. You're driving me crazy. What did the doctor say?"

"Ican'thavesexanymore," she said in a rush of words.

Ted's frown deepened. "I didn't catch any of that. Could you go a little slower?"

"Oh, dear. Okay. Ted, I can't have sex anymore. I'm no longer allowed to make love from now until about six weeks after the baby is born."

He nodded. "And?"

Hannah blinked. "And what? That's it. The bad news, the gruesome bulletin, the it's-been-great-but-goodbye announcement."

"Man, you've really lost me here, Ms. Doodle. Did I miss something? Goodbye? Who's leaving for where?"

"*You're* leaving," she said, nearly shrieking.

Ted's eyes widened. "*I* am? Why? Where am I going?"

"Out of my life," she said, pulling her hands free. She flapped one hand in the air. "You're gone. Poof. You're outta here."

"You're sending me away?"

"No, no, no, but why would you stay? My gosh, Ted, look at me. I'm as big as an inner tube and heading toward life raft. My feet are swollen by the end of the day, I waddle worse than Donald Duck, I wear tents instead of clothes and now I can't even make love." She sniffled. "I understand, I really do. So goodbye. I can't talk about this anymore or I'll cry."

Ted lunged to his feet to tower over her, his hands planted on his hips.

"We damn well *are* going to talk about this. I've never been so insulted in my life. You're really ticking me off, Hannah Johnson."

"I am?" she said, shock evident on her face. "I am *not*. I'm being realistic and mature. If I don't burst into tears, I will have accepted the facts with dignity and class.''

''Facts? Facts! You don't have facts, you have a bunch of bull!''

''Don't yell at me!''

''Well, hell, what do you expect me to do?''

''Leave!''

Ted groaned and shoved both hands through his hair. He stared at the ceiling and counted aloud to ten.

''Okay, I'm calm.'' He sat back down. ''Cool. Collected. In control. I won't yell. I won't tell you you're nuttier than a fruitcake, even though you are. Have you been binging on green grapes again? You're really wacko.''

''You're babbling.''

''And you're crazy!'' He shook his head. ''No, I won't raise my voice.'' He took her hands again. ''Hannah, listen to me, and please hear every word I'm saying. Are you paying attention?''

''Yes, but...''

''Please just listen, and don't interrupt.'' When she nodded, he continued, ''Ah, Hannah, what you said really hurt. Do you think I'm a sex maniac, or something? We can't make love anymore. Okay, I can live with that. I can still hold you in bed, rub your back when its aching, tell you how cute your toes look because you can't see them.''

He shifted his hands to frame her face.

''Hannah, the only way I'd leave you is if you sent me away, which would tear me apart. You surely realize I haven't seen anyone but you all these months, because I've obviously spent every spare minute with you. I don't want anyone but you.''

''It has been wonderful,'' she said, struggling against threatening tears. ''I've been so happy with you, and I've enjoyed every minute of the time we've spent together and with all the MacAllisters. They've made me feel like one of the family. And you've made me feel special, cherished and beautiful.''

''Because you *are* special and beautiful. You *should* be cherished, and I do. And I love you and—'' Ted stopped speaking and stiffened. ''What?'' he said.

''What?'' Hannah echoed.

''I...well, I'll be damned.'' A grin broke across his face. ''I do. I love you, Hannah Johnson. I, Theodore Sharpe, am in love with you.''

Hannah's eyes widened. ''You are not.'' She leaned back a bit, forcing him to drop his hands from her face. ''Don't you dare say such a thing.''

''I have to say it, because it's true. I wonder when it happened? This love stuff is sneaky. Man, oh, man, I'm in love. Hannah, you look like I just told you that Daisy had fourteen kittens in the middle of your bed. You're as pale as a ghost.''

''I... I don't want you to be in love with me,'' she said, her voice trembling. ''We were doing fine as we were. Everything was in its proper slot. Don't be in love with me, Ted. Please? Erase it, ignore it, make it go away.''

His smile faded and was replaced by a frown. ''I don't think I can do that.'' He shook his head. ''No, that's impossible. Love is a heavy-duty emotion,

Hannah. When it gets you, it gets you, a done deal. A person can't take two aspirin for it and feel better in the morning. I've never been in love before, but I can tell I don't have any control over it.''

''Oh, dear me,'' she said, shaking her head. ''This is terrible, just awful.''

''Thanks a lot, Ms. Doodle.''

''Oh, I'm so sorry, Ted. That sounded as though having you in love with me is a grim truth to be endured. That's not what I'm saying at all. It isn't personal. I just don't want *anyone* to be in love with me. Because it's you, and because I'm with you all the time, I'll have to figure out how I feel about *you,* and I don't want to do that.''

''Why not?''

''Because everything was perfect the way it was, don't you see?''

''What I see by the clock is that I have to get to work. I hate to put this discussion on hold, Hannah, but duty calls. I'll change into my uniform, then walk you home on the way to the elevator.'' He picked up the remote control and handed it to her. ''Watch the movie and find out if the good guy wins.''

He got to his feet, then leaned down and brushed his lips over hers.

''Until we can talk again after I wake up tomorrow,'' he said, close to her lips, ''don't think. Have you got that? You'll get yourself smack-dab in the middle of a major stress attack if you dwell on this. Okay? Promise me you'll at least try not to think?''

Hannah nodded, unable to speak due to the ache of unshed tears in her throat. She watched Ted leave the room, then took a shuddering breath.

Don't think, she told herself. *Oh, please, Hannah, don't think.*

Ted stood under the spray of hot water in the shower, mentally repeating his own directive like a mantra.

Don't think, Sharpe.

Don't think.

He could not, would not, dwell on the discovery that he was in love with Hannah Johnson, not now, not when he was about to go on duty.

Oh, Lord, he was in love.

How in the hell had that happened? He kept in touch with himself, knew how he felt about things, what his reactions to events meant. How could a man suddenly find that he was deeply in love with a woman and not have been aware of his changing and growing feelings?

He sure hadn't been kidding when he'd told Hannah that love was sneaky. It was powerful, potent and . . . sneaky.

His first reaction had been shock that had shifted almost instantly to pure joy. An incredible warmth had suffused him, and he'd had the urge to shout his declaration of love from the rooftops.

But now?

It was really sinking in, and felt like a rough punch in the gut. He'd betrayed himself, broken his own vow made years before to never become seriously involved

with a woman, never fall in love and definitely never
entertain the idea of marriage.

Damn, what a mess.

He was in love with Hannah.

Mumbling several earthy expletives, he turned off
the water, left the shower and began to dry himself
with an oversize towel.

Don't think.

But how could he shut down his mind? The reali-
zation that he loved Hannah was beating against his
brain.

Ted left the bathroom and began to dress, a frown
knitting his eyebrows.

If he looked at the situation in the short term, it was
great, fantastic. His beautiful Ms. Doodle was everything and more that a man could ever hope to have in
a wife. The past months spent with her were the hap-
piest of his entire life.

And the baby? The baby had captured his heart. He
could hardly wait to see it, hold it. To be a father to
that child, that miracle, would be one of the greatest
gifts and honors he'd ever received.

The baby would be Hannah's and his. *His.* He
would love it as his own, watch it grow and blossom
like a wondrous flower that *he* was helping to nurture. Hannah would be his wife, he would be her husband, and the child now within her would be theirs.

But later? A few years down the road? The ugly
truth would rise to the surface and destroy everything. It would be time for another baby, a sister or
brother for the one they had.

But he couldn't give Hannah that child.

Because he wasn't a whole man.

"Damn it, Sharpe," he said aloud, "don't think. Not now."

Several hours later, Ryan drove the patrol car slowly down a residential street, automatically scanning the area for anything that appeared out of order.

"You're awfully quiet tonight, Ted," he said.

"What? Oh, I guess I don't have anything brilliant to say."

Ryan chuckled. "You rarely do, but that doesn't keep you from talking."

"Yeah, well..." Ted paused. "Ryan, are you and Deedee going to have another baby?"

"Where did that come from?"

"Just answer the question."

"Yes, we're planning on having two kids. Teddy is still a baby, so there's no rush. We'll probably talk about it in a year or so."

"What about Jenny and Michael? Their Bobby is getting to be a big boy."

Ryan nodded. "They're trying for another one. It just hasn't happened yet." He laughed. "Jillian says she and Forrest are finished producing little Mac-Allisters. They got three at once and that's it, thank you very much.

"Andrea hasn't said anything, but I have a feeling she'll get pregnant again, in spite of having twins already. She'd probably be thrilled out of her socks to have another set of twins. She's a natural-born mother."

"So is Hannah," Ted said. "I mean, granted, she hasn't even had her baby yet, but all you have to do i watch her with the MacAllister brood to know the mothering instincts are there."

"There's no doubt in my mind that she'll be a good mother," Ryan said. "She could probably handle a houseful."

"Yeah." Ted sighed. "Yeah, I know."

Ryan glanced over at him quickly, then redirected his attention to his driving.

"What's on your mind, Ted? Why the subject o who's having how many babies? And why are you so bummed-out? Are you and Hannah having prob lems?"

"No, we're doing fine," he said quietly.

"You sure seem happy together. At times, I actu ally forget that you're not the father of her baby. You hover over her, tell her to put up her feet, talk abou the baby clothes you two bought, the whole nine yards. Don't slug me, but I think you're in love with Hannah. I also believe you consider that baby yours."

Ted looked out the side window for several long seconds, then shifted his gaze to Ryan.

"You're right," he said. "I *am* in love with Han nah. I didn't intend to be, but I am. And the baby? Hell, it's mine. I didn't have anything to do with its conception, but it's mine and Hannah's."

"So what's the problem here?" Ryan said. "Marry the woman and give the kid your name from day one. Hannah's ex-husband relinquished his claim on that baby, so go for it, man."

"It's not that simple, Ryan."

"It sure sounds simple to me. Unless..." Ryan's voice trailed off.

"Unless what?"

"Hannah doesn't love *you*. No, that's nuts. The whole family has seen you two together. She's in love with you. That's a given. Has she told you she loves you?"

"No."

"Well, be patient. You know she's been badly hurt in the past, and her idea was to never trust her judgment about a man again. You're the real goods, Ted. I bet she realizes that but is wary, afraid to say it out loud. Is *that* why you're bummed? Because Hannah hasn't said she's in love with you?"

"No. Let's change the subject."

"But—"

"This discussion is over and out, MacAllister."

"Well, hell."

Early the next afternoon, Hannah said goodbye to one of her piano students, then began to close the door.

"Hold it," Ted called from down the hall.

He sprinted to her door, stopped, then stepped into the living room. Hannah closed and locked the door behind him. As she turned to look at him, their eyes met and neither moved, nor spoke.

He was in love with this woman, Ted thought.

He wanted to spend the rest of his life with her, sharing, caring, protecting her.

He wanted to make love to her at night and know she'd be next to him each morning.

He wanted to be a father to her child, the baby sh
carried within her that he loved as his own.

He wanted to ask her now, right now, to be his wi
until death parted them.

Oh, how very much he wanted in regard to Hanna
Johnson.

But none of it was his to have.

"So," he said, managing to smile, "how's life?"

Hannah blinked, bringing herself from the haz
place she'd floated to while being held immobile b
Ted's mesmerizing blue eyes.

How's life? her mind echoed.

"How's life?" she said aloud, none too quietly. "A
in, 'What's cookin', toots?' You announce that yo
love me, tell me not to think, which is like ordering
person not to breathe, then breeze in here as cocky a
you please and say, 'How's life?' You have a lot o
nerve, Ted Sharpe."

Ted nodded. "Got it. You're not in a daffodils-and
daisies mood."

"Not even close." She moved around him and
crossed the room to lower herself onto the sofa in
not-very-graceful maneuver. "If I get any bigger," sh
muttered, "I'll need a crane to get up from here."

Now what? Ted wondered, turning slowly to look
at her. He didn't know what to do or say, how to han
dle this. Damn, if only he hadn't told Hannah that he
loved her. She was right; everything had been perfect
until he'd blown it by opening his big mouth.

No, correct that. It wasn't perfect.

Perfect would be to hear Hannah declare her love
for him, then accept his proposal of marriage.

Perfect would be raising the baby, then creating another one together in a few years.

Perfect wasn't going to happen.

Hannah smoothed her dress over her protruding stomach, averting her eyes from Ted's.

She had to quit screaming like a shrew, she told herself. It wasn't Ted's fault that his telling her he loved her had terrified her at the very same time that it filled her with the greatest joy she'd ever known.

It wasn't Ted's fault she was a befuddled, confused basket case.

It wasn't Ted's fault that she'd thought and thought, even though she'd tried so hard not to, had gotten in touch with herself and discovered . . .

Oh, dear heaven, discovered that she loved Theodore Sharpe with every breath in her blimp-size body.

"I'm . . . I'm sorry I yelled," she said, then slowly raised her eyes to look at him.

"Don't apologize. You had every right to holler." He went to the opposite end of the sofa and slouched onto the cushion.

Was this it? Hannah thought. Was this where Ted said he wanted to marry her? It was the natural order of things—*I love you and want you to be my wife.*

But what about the baby? Ted seemed enchanted with the idea of the baby. He'd made it clear that he wished to be involved in every aspect of her pregnancy, and all the preparations necessary for the baby's arrival.

Loving her meant loving the baby, too, and she knew, just somehow knew, that Ted realized that.

She knew what Ted was thinking and feeling? She, of the lousy track record, was presuming, assuming, deciding that this man was honest and real? She was out of her tiny mind.

And she loved Ted so very much.

Oh, what a mess. And, oh, mercy, what was she going to do and say if the next words out of Ted's mouth were a proposal of marriage?

"Well," Ted said, then sighed.

Get ready, Hannah, she told herself. Gear up. This was it.

"Well," he said again, "hell."

Hannah's eyes widened. "Hell? Oh." Was she disappointed? Relieved? Why didn't she know? Hell?

Ted shifted to face her, a frown on his face. "Hannah, do you love me?"

"Yes," she heard herself say.

That was great, just dandy, she fumed. He'd caught her off guard and she'd answered the question honestly, by reflex, as calmly as though he'd asked her if she wanted another slice of pizza. This situation was going from bad to worse, *very* quickly.

"I see," he said. "You love me."

Hallelujah! his mind sang. Hannah loved him! Hannah Johnson, his beautiful Ms. Doodle, was in love with him.

That was fantastic.

No, that was *not* good, not good at all.

She loved him and she knew he loved her. The next thing on the agenda should be to discuss getting married. But he couldn't marry Hannah; she deserved more than he was. She deserved a husband who was a whole man.

"Look," he said, "we love each other and we both love that baby. You *do* know how I feel about the baby, don't you?"

Hannah nodded, her gaze riveted on his face.

"We...um...have a nice routine worked out," he went on. "My duty shifts don't cause a problem with your giving piano lessons, because I have my own apartment where I can sleep at odd hours. We cook together, spend the evening together, sleep together, there, here, wherever the mood strikes. It seems to me that our loving each other..."

Damn it, he thought, he hated this. He couldn't leave her, not yet. He had to see her safely through the birth of the baby. Then he'd go, give her the opportunity to find a man who could give her everything she deserved to have. But what he really wanted was to marry her!

"Yes?" Hannah said, leaning slightly toward him. "Our loving each other...what?"

"Shouldn't change anything," he said, feeling a knot tighten in his gut. He shrugged. "We'll just keep on keeping on...exactly as we're doing."

"Oh, well..." Hannah waved one hand in the air. "Sure. You bet. That sounds just fine, Ted."

Yes, it was the best plan, she told herself. Now she didn't have to worry if loving Ted was another of her mistakes in judgment. It wasn't as though she was going to marry the man, for Pete's sake. If she was wrong about him, it would be much easier to deal with under the structure of their relationship as it now stood.

It was really a splendid idea, no doubt about it.

Then why did she feel as though her heart were splintering into a million pieces?

Chapter Ten

Thanksgiving, Ted thought, standing in front of the bathroom mirror to adjust his tie. It hardly seemed possible that the holiday season was already here.

Ted left the bathroom, then looked at his watch.

There was plenty of time before he and Hannah were due at the senior MacAllisters home for the traditional gathering of the clan for the Thanksgiving feast. This year, the event would also include celebrating Teddy's first birthday.

Thanksgiving, Ted mentally repeated as he wandered aimlessly around the living room.

He and Hannah had watched the parades on television that morning. No, that wasn't quite accurate. Hannah had watched the parades, while he'd watched Hannah watching the parades. He hadn't been able to take his eyes off her, nor curb his smile. She'd been like an enchanted little girl, her dark eyes sparkling, her continual "Oh, look, Ted, look" an absolute delight.

She was something, all right, his beautiful Ms. Doodle, and he loved her more with every passing day.

Ted's glance fell on the telephone and he replayed in his mind the conversation he'd had earlier with his parents. Thanksgiving greetings had been exchanged, along with the usual chitchat about his job, their leisure activities and the weather.

He had not said one word to his folks about the existence of Hannah Johnson in his life.

What was the point?

Why tell them he was in love for the first time?

Why tell them that Hannah had stolen his heart and there was no way possible he could ever get it back?

Why tell them that a baby, a miracle, was to be born with the coming of the New Year, a baby that in his heart, mind and soul was his?

What was the point, when he knew that after Hannah gave birth, he would be moving to another apartment, away from the building, out of her life?

Why explain that, because he loved her so deeply, he had to leave?

"Oh, man," Ted said aloud, dragging his hands down his face. Too restless to sit down, he went into the spare bedroom to stand in front of the worktable.

The dollhouse was just about finished. He had a few more touches of paint and stain to apply, then he'd assemble it and place the furniture in the rooms.

He enjoyed the project, but the closer he came to completing it, the more he wondered why he bothered to spend countless hours laboring over it. It would sit there gathering dust between rare visits from one or more of the MacAllister little girls.

Ted picked up one of the pieces—the framework and the front door of the house. He'd carved an intricate pattern on the door, then stained it dark and glossy.

He opened and shut the door several times, nodding in satisfaction that it moved smoothly back and forth.

A dollhouse, he mused, putting the piece back on the table. A doll *home?* No, it was a house, because there were no people. There would be walls, rooms, a roof and furniture, but as yet there wasn't a toy family to take up residence, to make it a home.

He had to decide if he'd make the figures, or buy them. He also had to decide when he would add the family, thus changing the house to a home.

A family. A mother, father and two babies. Two. Not one child, but two.

Ted closed his eyes for a moment, shook his head, then opened his eyes again and left the room.

He sat down on the sofa, leaned his head back and stared at the ceiling.

For years, he thought, he'd buried and ignored the truth of his inability to father a child. Now? The harsh reality was with him every day, tormenting him, haunting him, forcing him to accept his inadequacy and the ultimate price he was to pay for it.

He was going to lose Hannah and the baby.

One night when he'd been unable to sleep, he'd gently rested one hand on Hannah's stomach as she slept peacefully beside him. He'd savored each precious time he'd felt the baby move.

He'd fantasized about telling Hannah the truth, mentally supplied her with a smile, a shrug and the words, "Oh, well, no problem, Ted. We'll have one baby and Daisy the cat. You can't give me another child? Don't stress. It's no big deal."

He had jerked his hand away from Hannah's body, from the baby, and left the bed, trying to escape from the pain of knowing it *was* a problem, it *was* a big deal.

But there was nowhere to run or hide from the crushing truth, from reality.

Thanksgiving, he thought, with Christmas close behind, then the New Year, the birth of the baby, then . . .

Nothing.

Just emptiness.

Loneliness, cold and dark.

Ted shifted forward to rest his elbows on his knees, sinking his head into his hands.

"Ah, Hannah," he said, his voice raspy with emotion, "I love you so damn much."

He was jolted from his misery by the sound of the piano being played at full volume. He jerked his head up and listened.

"'Yankee Doodle,'" he said, recognizing the song. He looked at his watch. "Yes, ma'am, Ms. Doodle, I read you loud and clear, very loud. It's time to get going."

He grabbed his sport coat from the back of a chair nd left the apartment, anticipating the moment when lannah would open the door and greet him with a mile on her face and love shining in her incredible, big ark eyes.

And she did, along with the addition of her laugh-r, which made Ted's smile grow even bigger.

"You got my message," she said, stepping back so e could enter. "I wondered if playing 'Yankee Doo-le' would accomplish the job of bringing you over ere."

"It certainly did." He encircled her with his arms nd drew her as close to him as the baby allowed. You look beautiful, Ms. Doodle."

"Thank you. I thought burnt orange was an ap-ropriate shade to wear for Thanksgiving. It's an au-imn color."

"Mmm," he said, then captured her lips with his.

Hannah welcomed the kiss, parting her lips so Ted's ongue could slip between to seek and find her tongue, roking it in a sensuous duel.

She filled her senses with his aroma of woodsy af-r-shave, soap and man, savored the feel of his pow-ful body, and the taste of his mouth molded so erfectly to hers. She could hear the rapid tempo of er heart echoing in her ears.

Ted reluctantly raised his head and had to draw a ep breath before he could speak.

"Ready for some turkey and all the trimmings?" he id finally.

Hannah nodded. "I'm really hungry. I'll probably ake a piggy of myself." She paused. "Ted, we still

have a few minutes before we have to go. I'd like
talk to you. All right?''

"Sure." He released her, then grasped one of b
hands. "Come with me to the sofa, my dear."

Hannah laughed. "No, I'll sit in the straight ch.
so we don't have to use up an extra ten minutes p
ing me out of those puffy cushions."

"Oh, okay," he said, chuckling.

He sat down on the sofa and Hannah settled or
the chair. Daisy jumped up next to Ted.

"Hey, big stuff," he said, scratching her under t
chin. Daisy purred and closed her eyes. "You make
up here in a single bound now." He patted her on t
head, then looked at Hannah. "You have the flo
Ms. Doodle. You can have the ceiling and walls, tc
if you want them."

Hannah smiled, then became serious.

"Ted," she said, meeting his gaze, "my gran an
had traditions on Thanksgiving. We watched the p
rades on television, then cooked dinner together. E
fore we ate, we would talk about what we we
thankful for. Gran said it wasn't just a day for p
rades and lots of fancy food, it was a time to stop, ta
inventory and give thanks for our blessings."

Ted nodded. "That's nice. It sounds exactly li
something your gran would say."

"Well, I did that today, stopped and took inve
tory. I want you to know..." She took a steadyi
breath and lifted her chin. "I want you to know tha
not only love you, but I believe in you, trust you a
have no shadows of doubt about whether or not y
really are who you present yourself to be."

A chill swept through Ted and a painful knot twisted in his gut.

"For the first time in my life," she went on, "I've chosen well. I haven't made a mistake about the man I love, the one who holds my heart in his hands for safekeeping. For that, I'm very grateful and felt that today, Thanksgiving, was an appropriate time to tell you."

Oh, dear Lord, Ted thought, what had he done? Hannah's words were beautiful, a precious gift to be treasured. She'd moved past her fears and was now prepared to go forward with her life.

She loved him. Believed in him. Trusted him.

And she was making a terrible mistake.

He had a dark secret that he had knowingly kept from her. And because of that, he was going to hurt her, just as the men in her past had done, the ones she'd chosen to love and trust.

He couldn't bear the thought of Hannah's disillusionment because of him. She'd feel betrayed yet again, because of him. She'd blame herself, restore power to her fears, and resurrect her ghosts, because of him.

Oh, God. He had to tell her the truth about himself now, *right now,* Ted declared to himself. He had to tell her that he couldn't give her a baby, and because he loved her so very much, he had to leave her so she could find a man to love who could give her more children. He was lying to her with his silence.

But what if... The thought came to Ted suddenly. Could it be possible that Hannah would still love him, agree to marry him and spend the rest of her life with

him if she knew the truth? Would the child she no[w]
carried be enough to fulfill her maternal needs, h[er]
nurturing nature?

Or... would she consider adopting a child? Mayb[e]
two or three... Hell, a houseful of little ones wh[o]
needed love, and a home, and parents who woul[d]
consider them their own? Oh, man, Ted thought, th[at]
would be fantastic. They'd buy a big house and [it]
would ring with the joyous sound of children's laug[h]ter.

"Ted?" Hannah said, bringing him from his ra[c]ing thoughts.

"What? Oh, I'm sorry, Hannah. I was digestin[g]
what you said."

Hannah frowned. "You don't look too please[d]
about it. I thought... well, I thought you'd be happ[y]
to hear that I love you totally, with absolutely no re[s]ervations or doubts. I also believe that you love m[e]
and the baby in the same way."

"I do," he said quickly. "Oh, yes, Hannah, I d[o]
love you and the baby."

Tell her the truth! his mind hammered. *Lay it all o[ut]
there and pray.*

"I'm honored that you believe in me," he said[,]
"and trust in me. I really am." *Damn it, Sharpe, te[ll]
her.* "Thank you, Hannah."

She smiled at him warmly. "You're welcome."

I want to marry you, Ted Sharpe, her mind sang[.]
*spend my life with you, raise this baby together, as we[ll]
as the babies we'll have in the future. Ask me to b[e]
your wife, Ted. Ask me so I can say yes, yes, yes.*

"Hannah, I..." Ted's voice trailed off. A trickle of sweat ran down his back. No, he couldn't do it, not yet. It was too risky. What if he lost his Hannah? What if he saw disappointment on her face, then disgust, then the warm love in her eyes turn cold as she sent him away forever? No! "I think we'd better hit the road. If we don't get going, we'll be late."

He got to his feet and glanced around.

"Where's our birthday present for Teddy?" he said. "I swear, that stuffed toy beagle we got him looks exactly like nutso Scooter. Ryan is picking up my share of the wine for dinner when he gets his. Oh, you're taking fruit salad. Right? Come on, Hannah, we've got to be on our way."

Hannah looked at him intently, wishing she could peer into his brain.

She nodded, got to her feet, then headed toward the kitchen to retrieve the salad from the refrigerator.

Ted was acting strangely, she thought. He was talking too fast, wasn't looking directly at her and appeared suddenly nervous and edgy.

Should she have kept silent about believing in him, trusting him? She thought he'd be pleased to know she'd dealt with her ghosts and her fears; she had put them to rest at long last.

She was the one who had panicked when he'd first told her he loved her. She'd begged him not to love her, just erase those emotions like chalk from a blackboard. *Things were perfect as they were,* she declared at the time. *So couldn't they just continue on status quo?*

Ted had agreed, but she'd felt as though she'd le
him down, hadn't been able to give to him what h
wanted, needed and deserved to have.

But now?

Now they could have it all—a future, family, fo
ever love—that would withstand the rigors of time.

When Ted had agreed to leave the structure of thei
relationship as it was, she'd thought he was compro
mising, settling for less than he'd hoped to have. Ha
he since realized that the way things were suited hi
just fine? Did he intend to assume his Profession;
Uncle role in regard to her baby?

What was Ted thinking? Feeling?

They had to sit down and have a long talk, com
municate, have questions asked and answers given, sh
decided. But there wasn't time for that today.

"Yo, Ms. Doodle," Ted said. "We're going to b
unfashionably late."

"I'm coming. Teddy's gift is in the linen close
Would you get it, please?"

"Sure. Hey, Daisy, want us to bring you a big ol
drumstick?"

Several hours later, the scrumptious meal had bee
consumed, the kitchen cleaned, and to everyone
amazement, all the little ones were taking naps at th
same time. The family would celebrate Teddy's birth
day after the children had rested and were once agai
bundles of energy.

"Football-game time," Michael said. "I'm head
ing for the family room."

"Whoa," Forrest said. "There's important business to tend to first."

"Uh-oh," Andrea said. "I'm getting vibes about The Baby Bet."

"Oh, dear," Hannah said, laughing. "Don't you think there's too much other betting going on today, Forrest?"

"As the champion of The Baby Bet, I can put it into action when I so decree." He pressed one fingertip to the middle of his forehead. "Ah, yes, it's time to make my unbeatable prediction." He whipped a pen and a small notebook out of his shirt pocket. "Get your money ready, people. Crisp twenty-dollar bills. I don't take credit cards."

"Margaret," Robert MacAllister said, "your son is extremely obnoxious about The Baby Bet."

"*Your* son," she said, "has a head about the size of Toledo because he has never lost The Baby Bet. So *please* give very serious consideration to your prediction."

"Get as serious as you want to, Dad," Forrest said, "but I'll still win. What can I say? I'm an ace at this."

"Honey," Jillian said, smiling, "you're going to have a lot of crow to eat one of these days."

"Never happen, my sweet," Forrest said. "Okay, here's my bet. Hannah will have a boy on New Year's Day."

"Nope, nope, nope," Andrea said. "Hannah's baby is a smart cookie. He'll arrange to be a tax deduction for all of this year. I'm betting it's a boy on New Year's Eve. He'll be born on December thirty-first."

"Got it," Forrest said, recording his sister's bet on the pad of paper.

"No," Robert said, "a boy on my birthday, January fifth."

"A girl on New Year's Day," Michael said.

"No way," Ryan said. "He won't want to share the limelight with a holiday. He's going to be his own man. Twenty bucks on a boy on January second."

"Check," Forrest said, scribbling away. He glanced around the room. "Anyone else?"

No one spoke.

"All right," Forrest said, "all bets are recorded and—"

"A baby girl," Ted said quietly. "She'll be born on . . . on Christmas."

Hannah turned to look at Ted, her eyes widening. "Christmas?"

Ted nodded. "Yes. She'll arrive on Christmas. It's a girl with dark, silky hair like yours. We'd better have a present for her under the tree. It would be very tacky not to have a gift for someone you know is coming for Christmas. Did you write that down, Forrest?"

"Yup. Kiss your twenty goodbye, Sharpe."

Ted looked directly into Hannah's eyes. "Not this time. I know what I know."

"You really believe that you're right," Hannah said, an incredulous tone to her voice.

"Ms. Doodle . . ." Ted leaned forward and brushed his lips over hers. "It's guaranteed."

"Goodness," Deedee said, "you've convinced me, Ted. Ryan, withdraw your bet. You just threw away twenty dollars."

"All bets are final," Forrest said, flipping the notebook closed. "Ted, my boy, it will be a pleasure taking your money. I had the market cornered on being cocky about The Baby Bet, but you're outshining me here, you arrogant bum."

Ted just grinned at him.

"Cut it out," Forrest said. "You're making me nervous."

"*You're* nervous?" Hannah said, laughing. "I adore Christmas. I love opening presents and eating all the goodies, singing carols, everything that goes with the day. I wasn't planning on having a baby instead."

"Sorry, ma'am," Ted said, "but that's how it is. We'll celebrate Christmas a day late. No problem."

"Enough, enough," Andrea said, flapping her hands in the air. "You're giving me goose bumps, Ted. Hannah, have you chosen names for the baby yet?"

"If it's a girl, I want to name her after my gran, Patricia Elizabeth, and call her Patty. I haven't decided on a boy's name yet."

"You won't need one," Ted said. "Patty." He nodded. "Patricia Elizabeth. Patty. Nice, very nice."

Patty Sharpe, Hannah thought wistfully. Patricia Elizabeth Sharpe. It sounded absolutely perfect.

"Football," Michael said, getting to his feet.

Patty Sharpe, Ted thought. Patricia Elizabeth Sharpe. Mr. and Mrs. Theodore Sharpe and their daughter, Patricia Elizabeth, cordially invite... *Sharpe, shut up.*

"Football," Ted echoed.

"Bye," Hannah said, waggling her fingers at him.

"Don't you want to watch the game?" Ted said.

"Well, it's tempting. There are some very nice tushes displayed by those tight pants the players wear. But then they totally gross me out by spitting all the time. Spit, spit, spit. Their poor mothers must be mortified when they see that."

Ted hooted with laughter and joined the male exodus from the room. Hannah watched him go, a soft smile on her lips. When she turned her head again, her gaze collided with Deedee's.

"Patricia Elizabeth . . . Sharpe?" Deedee said.

"No, Deedee," Hannah said quietly, "I don't believe so." She splayed one hand on her stomach. "I think this is Patricia Elizabeth Johnson."

"Time will tell, dear," Margaret said. "Men, bless their silly hearts, are very unpredictable."

"Amen to that," Jillian said.

"You'd better have a boy's name ready, Hannah," Andrea said. "Forrest has never lost The Baby Bet, you know, and he says you're having a boy."

"Then it's a boy," Jenny said. "Forrest just doesn't lose The Baby Bet. You'll have a boy on New Year's Day, just as he predicted."

"Time will tell," Margaret repeated. "Babies are just as unpredictable as men."

"Uh-oh," Jillian said. "I hear little voices from down the hall. I think the troops are waking up. I'm going to convince the triplets that they want to watch football with their daddy."

"Good idea, Jillian," Deedee said. "I'll plunk Teddy in Ryan's lap, too. We'll let the daddies chase them around the family room for a while."

As Deedee, Jillian, Andrea and Jenny left the room to collect the children, a wave of chilling loneliness swept over Hannah.

A daddy, she thought, resting her hands on her stomach in a protective gesture. She'd hoped, more than she'd even realized at the time, that telling Ted she trusted and believed in him, knew she had finally chosen the right man to love, would bring a smile to his face, then a change in the structure of their relationship.

She wanted to marry Ted Sharpe.

She wanted the baby to have Ted as her daddy.

But he had acted so strangely when she made her grand announcement that she'd counted her blessings, per the Thanksgiving tradition her gran had taught her. He'd seemed uncomfortable and suddenly nervous as she told him she now knew he was exactly who he presented himself to be.

Then she'd decided they needed to sit down and talk things through, communicate, share their thoughts and feelings.

But now? During the hours since that scene in her apartment, she was having second thoughts about the idea of a serious discussion with Ted. He knew how she felt, where she was emotionally. What more could she say that he didn't already know? Nothing.

The ball, as the cliché went, was in Ted's court. Her future, the baby's future, were in his hands. Did he want to be a husband and father? Or would he be satisfied with the roles of lover and Professional Uncle?

She didn't know. She just didn't know what Ted really wanted.

"Hannah," Margaret said gently, bringing her out of her reverie, "I feel I need to say this again. Time will tell."

Hannah managed to produce a weak smile as she nodded her agreement, unable to speak as unshed tears closed her throat.

Late that night, Deedee wiggled close to Ryan in their bed.

"Ryan," she said, poking him on the arm, "are you awake?"

"I am now," he mumbled.

"This is important. Has Ted given you any indication, even the slightest hint, that he intends to ask Hannah to marry him?"

"No."

"Have you asked him about it?"

"No."

"Why not?"

"If he had something to tell me, he'd tell me. Good night, Deedee."

"Men. Good grief, if a woman wants to know what another woman is thinking, she asks her. Couldn't you sort of nudge Ted toward the subject of his marrying Hannah and see what he says?"

"No. Good night, Deedee."

"But, Ryan, he's obviously in love with Hannah, and he's thrilled to pieces about that baby. Why doesn't he make them all a family, marry Hannah, give the baby his name? What on earth is that man's problem?"

"Deedee?"

"Yes?"

"Good night!"

"Well, darn. Good night, Ryan."

Chapter Eleven

Immediately after Thanksgiving, merchants rushed to transform their stores into Christmassy fairylands, hoping to entice holiday shoppers.

Everyone took deep, fortifying breaths and began to make endless lists of what needed to be accomplished to assure wonderful celebrations, and then rolled their eyes heavenward as they envisioned the balances due on credit cards in January.

Ted, Ryan and police officers across the country geared up for hectic work shifts, knowing the crime rate would increase in the frenzy, as it did each year.

The MacAllisters, like many large families, drew names for gift giving among the adults, while agreeing that presents should be bought for all the children.

At a bring-a-dessert-to-share gathering at Jillian and Forrest's two weeks after Thanksgiving, Robert Mac-Allister announced that he had put the names on slips of paper into a bowl, per the tradition, and the drawing would commence after the vast array of desserts were consumed.

Hannah frowned and leaned close to Ted, hoping the chatter taking place around the large table would muffle what she was about to say for Ted's ears only.

"Ted," she whispered, "you didn't tell me this get-together was for the purpose of drawing names for Christmas gifts. I shouldn't be here."

"Why not?" he said, matching her whisper.

"Because I'm not one of the family."

"Either am I, but I'm in the draw each year. You're considered part of the group, just as I am. I meant to tell you what we were going to do here tonight, but it slipped my mind."

"But—"

"Hey, you belong here, just as I do." He brushed a kiss over her lips. "Trust me."

"Mmm," she said, glowering at him.

Ted laughed, then directed his attention to Michael, who had just asked him a question.

Well, Hannah thought, so be it. She couldn't very well refuse to draw a name, nor ask that hers be removed from the bowl. She'd just sit back and savor being part of this marvelous family.

She took a bite of carrot cake and inwardly sighed.

What would be happening in her life a year from now? Would she and Ted still be together, as they now were; Ted living in his apartment, she in hers? Would

Ted be interacting with the baby in his favored role of Professional Uncle? Would her child be just another little one he lavished with attention before merrily going on his bachelor way?

There had been no serious discussion after Thanksgiving regarding her heartfelt announcement to Ted that she believed in him and trusted him. Ted had continued to be attentive, thoughtful and loving. She couldn't find fault with anything he'd said or done, but . . .

There was, Hannah knew, a seed of sadness within her that she hoped wouldn't grow bigger, all-consuming. She was trying, she really was, to view each dawn as a daffodils-and-daisies day, not dwell on her yearning to be Ted's wife.

She'd mentally scolded herself on more than one occasion, telling herself that she should count her blessings for what she had, not even be thinking about what was missing.

To have a wonderful man in her life who loved her and who loved a baby who had been fathered by someone else, was a rare gift to be cherished. She'd fully expected to be alone during and after her pregnancy. But Ted was there for her, as was the whole MacAllister family.

She *was* grateful, she truly was, but she was also human, with natural desires. She wanted to marry the man she loved. The man she loved with an intensity she never would have dreamed possible.

But it wasn't going to happen.

Nothing had changed since her declaration on Thanksgiving. Well, that wasn't entirely true. Ted emed to like saying, 'Trust me,' when it fit the cirumstances, because now he knew she did. But that as it—the only difference in their relationship beween before and after Thanksgiving.

Time will tell, Margaret MacAllister had said. Time as telling, all right, Hannah thought. Ted Sharpe had o intention of marrying Hannah Johnson, nor being real father to the baby. And the truth was making her d, so very, very sad.

"So, Hannah," Forrest said, bringing her from her oomy thoughts, "how's the New Year's Day baby ing? Been to the doctor lately?"

Hannah smiled. "Yes, I have, as a matter of fact. aid boy is turning and dropping right on schedule. osh, Forrest, when he's born on New Year's Day, do u suppose he'll be tossing confetti around the deery room?"

"Now, there's a thought," Forrest said. "It ouldn't surprise me at all."

"You're cooked, MacAllister," Ted said. "It's a rl, remember? Born on Christmas, remember? The aby Bet championship title is changing hands, reember? I have to decide what I'm going to buy with ose pretty twenty-dollar bills."

"Never happen, Sharpe," Forrest said, a *very* smug pression on his face. "Facts are facts when it comes The Baby Bet. I can't be beat." He leaned forward d peered at Hannah's stomach. "Yo, Baby Dooe, this is Uncle Forrest speaking. Don't let me down, ddo. I have my reputation, as well as my wallet, to otect."

"Your sanity could use some scrutiny," Jillian sa[id,] laughing. "Baby Doodle has a mind of his own."

"*Her,*" Ted said. "Girls are referred to as 'he[r,]' Jillian."

"Attention, attention," Robert MacAllister sa[id] suddenly. "It's time to do the deed. The rules are [the] same as every year. If you draw your own name, [or] your husband's, wife's—" he smiled at Hannah a[nd] Ted "—or significant other, put it back in the bo[x] and pull out another slip of paper."

"We should change that rule," Andrea said. "[I'd] love to buy myself a super Christmas present."

"You *do,*" said her husband, John. "You ev[en] wrap it and put a tag on it that says, To Andrea fr[om] Santa Claus."

"I know," she said, laughing. "But if I picked [my] own name, I could do it legally."

"Nope," Robert said, "the rules stand. You ca[n't] have your important person's name, either, becaus[e it] goes without saying that you'd better buy them a g[ift] if you want to live long enough to see Hannah's s[on] born on January fifth."

"Oh," Jillian said with a moan. "Please don't br[ing] up the subject of The Baby Bet again. Forrest is g[et]ting hard to live with."

"You're just figuring that out?" Michael sa[id.] "You're a tad slow on the uptake, Jillian. Forrest [has] been a pain in the tush since the day he was born."

"Children," Margaret said, smiling at their no[n]sense, "your father is speaking. Behave yourselves[.]"

"Thank you, Margaret," Robert said. "This is [se]rious business. There are only three weeks u[ntil]

hristmas. Prepare to shop, people.'' He picked up
ιe bowl. ''Let the ceremony begin.''

Robert moved around the table, bowing as he pre-
ᴇnted the bowl to each participant. Everyone was
ɔon laughing, talking and making grand perform-
ιces of hiding the name on their slip of paper.

Hannah drew Andrea's name, then turned to Ted.

''Who did you get?'' she asked him.

''My lips are sealed.''

''You won't even tell *me?* We're going Christmas
ιopping together.''

''Only to a point, Ms. Doodle,'' he said, grinning.
You won't be around when I buy a gift for the per-
ɔn on this slip of paper, *or* when I shop for you.''

''Phooey on you,'' Hannah said, poking her nose
ι the air.

''Well said,'' Deedee said.

''I'm macho and tough,'' Ted said. ''I can handle
ɔhooey on you.' ''

Just then, the telephone rang and Forrest went to
ιswer it. A few moments later, he yelled from the
ιtchen. ''Hey, Ryan, Ted, one of you guys come take
ιis call.''

''Uh-oh,'' Ryan said, getting to his feet.

''Oh, boy,'' Ted said, shaking his head.

Hannah looked at him. ''Do you think you're be-
ιg told to come back on duty?''

''Guaranteed. We're all on standby until after New
ᴇar's. We have to leave a number where we can be
ᴇached twenty-four hours a day. It's not just the sea-
ɔn to be jolly.''

Ryan strode back into the room. "Let's roll, par
ner. We've got a dozen cars or more in a pileup. Th
need traffic and crowd control, and reports written

"Oh, joy and rapture," Ted said. He gave Hann
a quick kiss, then swept his eyes over the gro
"Someone take Hannah home, okay? All the w
home. Don't just drop her off at the complex. See I
safely inside her apartment, and listen for the lock
snap into place."

"Yes, sir," Forrest said, saluting. "I understa
sir."

Ryan kissed Deedee, then Ryan and Ted hurri
from the room.

"Ah, the perks of being a police officer's wife
Deedee said. "Guess what, Hannah? You *don't*
used to this, or the worry that goes with the title,
ther. You just deal with it the best you can."

Hannah nodded absently, then conversation
sumed around the table.

Oh, she *was* learning to 'deal with it,' Hann
thought. But the glaring difference between hers
and Deedee, was that Hannah Johnson was *not* a p
lice officer's *wife*.

Late the next afternoon, an exhausted Ted enter
his apartment. He and Ryan had been kept bu
through the night, then had stayed on duty for th
assigned day shift. He'd telephoned Hannah befo
leaving the station, saying he was dead tired but fir
and would see her late that evening after he'd slept i
an hour or two.

He'd no sooner crawled naked between the cool
sheets on his bed and lowered his head to the inviting
pillow, when the telephone rang.

"Hell," he muttered.

He snatched up the receiver from the telephone on
the nightstand.

"What!" he said, his head still burrowed deep in the
pillow.

"Oh, dear," a woman said, "I woke you. I'm terribly sorry. Shall I call later?"

"Mom?" Ted said, jerking upward to a sitting position.

"Yes, it's your mother," Susan Sharpe said, laughing softly, "who knows from experience that a wise
person never wakes a sleeping baby. Tell me what time
I should call you back."

"No, no, I'm awake. I just got off a double shift
and hit the sheets, but I wasn't asleep yet. What's
goin'?"

"I'll make this quick so you can get your rest. Your
father and I have decided to come over there in the
motor home after Christmas.

"We'd love to spend the actual holiday with you,
but your aunt and uncle are joining us here on Christmas Day. We'll celebrate with you a couple of days
late."

Holy hell, Ted thought, his mind racing. His parents couldn't come for a visit. Hannah was here!

"We'll stay at that nice park that we discovered last
time we visited you," Susan went on. "We can hook
up the motor home to electricity, they have lovely
shower facilities, shuffleboard, all kinds of goodies.

We'll entertain ourselves and connect with you wi
you're off duty. How does all this sound to y
Ted?''

"It sounds...um," he started. Terrible. It wa
disaster in the making. Oh, man, what a mess. "Gr
just great.''

Susan laughed. "I'll chalk up your lack of ent
siasm to the fact that you're tired. Well, get so
sleep, my darling. I'll give you more details ab
when we're arriving after we've figured everything c
Your father and I are looking forward to seeing yo

"Oh, I'm...I'm eager to see you both, too. Y
You bet, Mom.''

"Goodbye for now, dear.''

"Yeah. Bye.''

Ted replaced the receiver, then sank back onto
pillow with a groan.

"Oh, man," he said, dragging his hands down
face. He dropped his arms to the bed with a thud.

"Mom, Dad," he said aloud, "this is Hannah, a
known as Ms. Doodle. That cute lump is her baby
love this woman and child, but don't get excited ab
it, because I'm walking out of Hannah's life right
ter the baby has arrived safely.

"Why? Because I can't give her *another* baby in
future. That's not fair to her. Get it? So, say hel
Hannah, then goodbye, Hannah, and be done w
it.''

Ted closed his eyes and moaned again.

"I don't believe this. What in the hell am I going
do?''

* * *

The next day, as Ted and Ryan were cruising in the patrol car through the parking lot of a large shopping mall, Ted sighed.

"Okay, Sharpe," Ryan said, "that's ten."

Ted looked over at Ryan, obviously confused. "Ten what?"

"Ten sighs, moans, whatever you want to call them. What's on your mind?"

Ted sighed.

"Eleven."

"Yeah, okay, okay. My folks are coming to visit right after Christmas."

"Oh? That's nice. They're good people, fun to be with. All the MacAllisters like them a lot. So far, I'm missing the problem here."

"Damn it, Ryan, how am I going to keep them from seeing and meeting Hannah?"

Ryan frowned. "Why would you want to?"

"Because... Oh, hell, forget it."

"Is there some reason that you think they wouldn't like or accept Hannah? And the baby?"

"No, they'd love her on sight. And the baby? My mom would be ecstatic. She'd run, not walk, to the nearest store for yarn so she could knit the baby something. It wouldn't matter to them if I was the father of that child or not. They'd be thrilled out of their socks that I was involved with Hannah. In fact, they'd know that I wasn't the..." His voice trailed off.

"Wasn't the what?"

"Nothing."

"The father of the baby?" Ryan said. "Come o
Ted, I know your folks. They're very together. Th
don't think for one minute that you're living like
monk. They might wonder why you haven't marri
Hannah, but.... Okay, I'm going for it. Ted, ever
one in the family can't figure out why you haver
married Hannah."

"Yeah, well, I go around with a twenty-four-hou
a-day knot in my gut because I have a feeling th
Hannah is wondering the same thing. She's just to
classy to come right out and ask me what the hold
is."

"*I'm* not that classy. Sharpe, why haven't yo
married Hannah?"

Ted shifted his gaze out the side window of the v
hicle.

"I can't," he said quietly.

Ryan glanced over at him quickly, then redirect
his attention to his driving. He left the parking lot an
drove into a residential area. The heavy silence in th
car was broken only by an occasional exchange ov
the radio.

"Want to talk about it?" Ryan said finally.

"No." Ted paused, then looked at Ryan. "Yeah,
think maybe I *would* like to talk about it. It's be
bottled up inside of me for so damn long, buri
where I didn't have to deal with it. Now, because
Hannah, I have to face it head-on and it's ripping n
up.

"The thing is, Ryan, I realize that you and Deed
share everything. I couldn't handle her knowing abo
this. It's going to be tough enough telling *you*."

"I give you my word that whatever you say is just between the two of us. Deedee would understand and respect that. You're hurtin', buddy. I can hear it in your voice. You've seen me through some really bad times, Lord knows. I'm here, I'll listen, if you want to talk."

Ted drew a shuddering breath.

"Ryan, I love Hannah so much. And that baby? I love her like she was my own. She *is* mine, in my heart, my mind. I can hardly wait to see her, hold her. She's a miracle. I feel her move, dance a jig inside Hannah, and I choke up. I'm awed by the wonder of her."

Ryan nodded but didn't speak.

"Sometimes," Ted went on, his voice raspy, "I allow myself to fantasize about marrying Hannah, the two of us raising the baby together in a nice house filled with love, laughter, daffodils and daisies. Man, what a beautiful picture that scenario is in my mind. Perfect. Absolutely perfect. Until..." He shook his head.

Ryan waited silently.

"Until," Ted continued, "it's time to consider having another baby. Then the dream vanishes, destroyed by the truth. Ryan, I'm...I'm sterile. I had the mumps when I was sixteen and it left me... I'm not a whole man. I can't give Hannah a baby, not ever. Now do you understand why I haven't asked her to marry me? Why I won't ever ask her?"

Ryan released a pent-up breath. "No."

"Hell. You can't possibly relate to how I feel. You fathered Teddy. You'll click off another kid when you decide you want one. Forget it. There's no sense in talking to you about this."

"Hold it, buddy. I listened and now I have the right to speak. Where is this 'I'm not a whole man' stuff coming from? Ted, a guy isn't measured by his sperm count!

"So, okay, you had the mumps and you're sterile because you did. It happens. That doesn't make you less of a man, not in the things that matter. I can't believe you have the attitude you do. What...or maybe it's who...made you come to this conclusion?"

"My father!"

"Dean Sharpe?" Ryan said, shock evident on his face and in his voice. "Your dad? I've known him for years and I can't... He said to your face that you weren't a whole man because you can't father a child?"

"No. No, I overheard him talking to my mom after the doctor called with the test results," Ted said, suddenly weary, totally exhausted. "I ran out of the house, ran as fast and as far as I could. My folks didn't know I was there when they were discussing it. Later, when they told me, I blew it off, said it was no big deal.

"My dad put his arm around me, said there were babies all over the world who needed homes, people to love them. I could get married and adopt kids. But I knew how he really felt about me. His precious son wasn't a whole man, never would be."

"You were sixteen years old. You could have misinterpreted what your father said to your mother.

Didn't you ever sit down with your dad and clear the air?''

''No. There was nothing more to say. Ever since then, there's something missing between me and my father. Things were never quite the same after that.''

''Oh, man,'' Ryan said, shaking his head.

''Time passed, I became a cop, a swinging-single bachelor to the max, then a Professional Uncle to the MacAllister kids. But then . . .''

''Hannah.''

Ted nodded. ''Hannah, my beautiful Ms. Doodle, and Patricia Elizabeth, the baby girl I'd sell my soul to hear call me Daddy.''

''Ted, don't you think Hannah has the right to make her own decision about this? You're deciding that you're not good enough for her. She has a mind, you know. Even more, she has a heart. She loves you, Ted.

''Tell her the truth. See how she feels about adopting, or just raising the one baby that's on the way. She's the other half of this scenario. She has the right to have a voice in this.''

''No. I can't tell her. I've left it too late. She's come to believe in me and trust in me. But I've lied to her with my silence. I'm no better than the other jerks who hurt her in the past.

''After the baby is born, I'm leaving. I'm getting out of her life so she can have what she deserves in a man. She'll find someone who can give her another baby.''

"Damn it, Ted, don't do this. You're making a terrible mistake. Go to Hannah, talk to her, tell her the truth."

"No!"

"Why in the hell not?" Ryan yelled.

"Because she loves me!"

Ryan opened his mouth, shut it again, then gave his head a sharp shake as though attempting to clear a sudden fog that had dropped over his brain.

"Did that make sense?" Ryan said. "No, it definitely did *not*. Want to run that by me again, Sharpe?"

"Not really, but I will. Look, Ryan, suppose, just suppose, that Hannah forgave me for withholding the truth from her. I doubt that she would, but let's pretend she did. The issue at the moment is truth, trust, not the subject matter of what I was withholding."

"Check."

"Then suppose she forgave me for not telling her when I should have. I never told her I wasn't a whole man, normal, capable of fathering children. But we'll suppose for now that she forgave me for my false front."

"The 'not a whole man' bit is still a crock, but for the sake of whatever point you're trying to make here...check."

"Okay. Now. Hannah loves me and because she does, she'd probably say that it was all right that I can't make babies. She'd agree to marry me and off we'd ride into the sunset with Patricia Elizabeth."

"Check."

"No, damn it, that's the glitch, not a check. Later, Ryan, down the road, when Patty is a little girl, no longer a baby, Hannah would feel robbed, unfulfilled, because she'd yearn for another baby. She'd smile, laugh, be sunny Ms. Doodle embracing daffodils-and-daisies days, but inside she'd be crying. She'd be crying, MacAllister, and I'd be the cause of that pain."

"No matter what she said to you," Ryan said, "you'd be certain that she was miserable."

"Yes."

"Check."

"There's no way for me to win here, Ryan, no matter what I do. I'm selfish enough to want to wait until the baby is born, to see her and hold her, then I know I'll have to leave. I don't have any other choice."

"You're right."

Ted blinked. "I am?"

"Oh, yeah, no doubt about it. Want to know why? Don't answer that, because I'm going to tell you whether you want to know or not.

"Hannah Johnson loves you. You love Hannah Johnson. The big difference is, she *knows* how to love. She trusts you, believes in you, all that good jazz.

"But you, Ted? You love Hannah, but you really don't know how to go about it. If you did, you'd tell her straight up that you're sterile, then discuss whether to raise Patty as an only child, or adopt.

"Yeah, Hannah trusts and believes in you. But guess what? *You* don't trust *her* to tell you what's really in her heart about this situation.

"So, I agree with you that you should leave her. Not because you can't father a child, but because you don't deserve the kind of love she's offering you. You, Sharpe, aren't giving her that same kind of love, that depth, in return."

"But—"

"So, yes, you're right, buddy," Ryan said, nodding. "As soon as that baby is born, you should hit the road."

Chapter Twelve

Ted lay stretched out on his back on Hannah's living-room floor, his hands beneath his head, eyes closed.

Daisy was curled on his chest, lulled into blissful sleep by the steady rise and fall of Ted's breathing.

Hannah was playing Christmas carols on the piano in the glow of the multicolored lights of the tree they'd decorated that evening.

This was, Ted mused, one of the most peaceful moments he'd had since his disturbing conversation with Ryan a week ago. The only reason he was completely relaxed and thoroughly enjoying the music was that he'd actually managed to shut down his mind and not think.

And he was *not* going to think for the remainder of the evening.

Got that, Sharpe? he asked himself. He'd been over the facts concerning his relationship with Hannah a thousand times, accomplishing nothing more than becoming extremely proficient at chasing around his own thoughts in a maddening circle.

Why he kept dwelling on the dilemma, he didn't know. It wasn't as though he was seeking an answer to the question of what he should do.

He knew what he had to do.

He was going to walk away from Hannah.

It was the proper course of action, the most loving and fair.

You're right, buddy, as soon as that baby is born, you should hit the road.

Ryan's words echoed in Ted's mind, and he opened his eyes and glowered at the ceiling.

Man, he'd hated hearing Ryan say that. The harsh reality of that statement had seemed to slice through him like a knife, causing him to flinch from the pain.

Ryan had done nothing more than agree with Ted's own theory and the conclusion he'd come to, but Ted's first reaction had been to want to angrily deny the accuracy of what Ryan had said, tell his partner he was nuts and should take a long walk off a short pier.

Leave Hannah? Never.

Oh, Lord, leave Hannah. He had to.

Damn it, Sharpe, don't think.

* * *

Hannah played "White Christmas" from memory, leaving her free to gaze at Ted where he was lying on the floor with Daisy.

Ted, Ted, Ted, she thought dreamily. She loved him. Oh, how very much she loved that magnificent man.

He'd shown up at her door early that evening with a Christmas tree and a shopping bag full of ornaments and lights.

When he'd inquired the week before about her plans for a tree, she'd told him that her ex-husband had taken the boxes of decorations, and her budget didn't allow for purchasing new ones. Next year, she'd have a small, pretty tree for the baby's first Christmas.

Then up popped Ted with a tree and all the trimmings, telling her that *this* was Patty's first Christmas. She was definitely here, he'd decided, giving Hannah's stomach a friendly pat. And besides, Patricia Elizabeth was going to be born on Christmas Day.

Such fun it had been decorating the tree with Ted. Such special memories she'd tucked carefully away in a cozy corner of her heart.

A wave of sadness suddenly swept through Hannah and she attempted to push it away, not allow it to linger.

She finished playing "White Christmas" and went on to "Silent Night," again knowing it from memory. It was her favorite Christmas carol, so hauntingly lovely. She felt threatening tears burning at the back of her eyes.

Oh, Hannah, she admonished herself. *Don't be sad.* No one got *everything* they wanted in life. Her desire to be Ted's wife, stay by his side in that role until death parted them, was a wish and prayer that was not hers to realize.

She could still be happy, she told herself, if she worked very hard on her outlook and attitude, approached the tomorrows as daffodils-and-daisies days. Ted would be there for her and the baby, just as he now was. That he wouldn't have the titles of husband and father were facts she had to handle and make all right as they stood.

I'll do it, Gran, she thought. *Somehow.*

Hannah played the last chords of "Silent Night," then lifted her hands from the keys. She leveled her bulky body upward and moved away from the piano.

"That was really nice," Ted said, still in his prone position.

"Thank you," she said, easing onto the straight-backed chair. "I would have played more, but my back hurts. I have to lean forward at a weird angle to reach the keys and I don't last long." She swept her gaze over the tree. "Oh, it's so pretty. Thank you, Ted."

He chuckled, causing Daisy to bounce on his chest. The kitten woke and began to wash one paw.

"You've thanked me forty-two times," Ted said. "Enough already."

"Okay. Then I'll thank you for buying gifts for the MacAllister kids for both of us to give them."

"You covered that one, too," he said, smiling. "You discovered that shopping in the crowds wipes you out, and your budget wasn't prepared to include a herd of munchkins. Elementary, my dear. I took care of it. Besides, I'm ready for any excuse to hang out in toy departments. That is really a kick. They've got dynamite stuff for sale this year.''

Ted lifted Daisy from his chest and placed her gently on the floor. He rolled to his feet, then sat down on the sofa. Looking over at the tree, he nodded in approval, then directed his attention to Hannah.

"How did your final childbirth class go last night?" he said.

"Fine, I guess. I can pant and puff with the best of them.''

Ted grinned. "I hope your friend Laurie won't mind having her Christmas interrupted. As your coach, she'll have to be there on the twenty-fifth when Patricia Elizabeth arrives.''

"I told her about The Baby Bet." Hannah laughed. "She's cheering for Forrest. She said her husband is a couch potato on New Year's Day, watching football, and it would be a perfect time for her to be with me at the hospital.''

"Well, too bad for Laurie, because *I'm* winning The Baby Bet this go-round. Hear that, Patty?" he said in a louder voice. "Christmas Day, kid. Don't let me down.''

"You're so crazy.''

Ted smiled, shrugged, then became serious.

"Hannah," he said, "my folks are coming over between Christmas and New Year's. They'll park their motor home at a camp near here and pop in and out of my place when I'm off duty.''

"Oh, how nice. You must be looking forward to seeing them.''

"Yeah, sure I am, but... Well, I thought I should prepare you because they'll be, you know, curious about what you and I... What I mean is, they'll wonder if we're... Damn."

Hannah cocked her head slightly to one side.

"Ted," she said, frowning, "are you saying you haven't told your parents that you're involved with a woman who's about to give birth to a baby?"

"No, I... um... I haven't mentioned it."

Hannah's eyes widened. "Good grief, what if they take one look at me and assume the baby is yours?"

It is! his mind yelled. In all the ways that mattered, the baby was his.

"Patty will already be born by the time they arrive, remember?" Ted's attempt at a smile failed.

"Born, not born, that isn't the point. Ted, why haven't you told them about me?"

Damn, he thought, what should he say? The lie he was *living* now was ripping him apart. He could not, would not, tell Hannah an out-and-out *spoken* lie.

"Look," he said, "my folks are great people, they really are. I'm not as close to my dad as I am to my mom, but..." He shrugged. "That's not unusual, I guess. The thing is, I'm their only child, so they...my mom especially... want to know the nitty-gritty of what's going on in my life. You know what I mean?

"Not that they pry, or get pushy about it, but one question leads to another, then another, so I just sort of keep my mouth shut about a lot of things. Get the drift? Anyway—"

"You're babbling."

"I am? Oh." He cleared his throat. "Well, I'll stop talking, then."

"You *do* intend to introduce me to them?"

"Yeah, sure. That's why I was warning you that they were coming."

"That's dandy," she said, throwing up her hands in frustration. "Let's see, how's this? It's a pleasure to meet you, Mr. and Mrs. Sharpe. You have a wonderful son, but this isn't his baby. Ted and I are lovers, but I was already pregnant when I met him by waking him playing 'Yankee Doodle' on the piano.

"I wanted to clear up the baby business right away so you wouldn't think your Theodore hadn't done the honorable thing after getting me pregnant. Okey-dokey, folks? Great. No problem."

Ted nodded. "That about covers it. I don't think you need to throw in the bit about us being lovers, though. My parents aren't stupid or prudish, but there's no reason to hit them over the head with it."

"Aaak!" Hannah yelled.

Ted jerked in surprise at her outburst.

"What!" he said, matching her volume.

"I was being sarcastic, you dope. I was attempting to make it clear that you can't produce a very pregnant woman out of the blue and expect your parents to just calmly sit down and have a chat about the weather."

"Oh."

"That's not fair to them, or to me, Ted. It's your responsibility to tell them about me *before* I meet them. If you don't, I'm going to be very uncomfortable and I'm certain they will be, too."

"Oh." He sighed. "All right, I'll take care of it."

"Well, I'm sorry it's such a burden on you." She folded her hands on her large stomach and lifted her chin, glaring at Ted for good measure.

"You're angry," he said.

"No. My feelings are hurt. You're treating me like this was the Victorian age, when they stuck the disgraceful pregnant female in the broom closet when guests came."

Ted got to his feet and crossed the room. He hunkered down next to Hannah's chair and covered her hands where they rested on her stomach with one of his own.

"You wouldn't fit in a broom closet," he said, producing his best hundred-watt smile.

"You," she said, turning her head to look at him, "are a dead man."

His smile instantly disappeared.

"Just a little humor there," he said. "Sorry. Hannah, I wouldn't hurt your feelings for the world. I was taking the easy road with my folks, that's all. My mom will want details, details, details, but I'll tell them about you before you meet them. I promise. Okay?"

Hannah nodded.

Ted stood, then shifted to stand in front of the chair. He braced his hands on the arms, then leaned over to claim Hannah's mouth in a searing kiss.

Hannah's lashes drifted down as she parted her lips to receive his tongue, savoring his taste as well as the heated sensations of desire that instantly swirled within her.

Oh, Ted, her mind hummed. She was so tired of being pregnant; fat and clumsy and unattractive. She wanted to be slender again, womanly. She wanted to make love through the night with the man she loved, with Ted.

Ted reluctantly broke the kiss and straightened.

"Whew," he said, taking a ragged breath. "You're potent stuff, Ms. Doodle."

"I'm fat stuff," she said miserably. "I've had enough of toting this load around and looking like a blimp, a life raft, a whale. I want to tie my own shoes, for crying out loud."

Ted chuckled. "I've heard MacAllister ladies sing that song. Isn't it nice to know you're normal? Hey, Christmas is only two weeks away. You're in the home stretch, my sweet."

"I know, but... Ted, do you realize you've never seen me *not* pregnant?"

"I hadn't thought about it, but you're right. So?"

"So, could we make a date now to go out to dinner after the baby is born and I get my figure back? I hope it doesn't take too long to have a flat tummy again. I'll wear a pretty dress, a slinky number, that announces 'I am woman,' and we'll do up the town. That would be so nice to look forward to."

"Ah, Hannah, the way you are right now declares you to be a woman to the maximum. You're so beautiful. I'm going to remember what you looked like pregnant, memorize every precious detail."

"Heaven forbid."

"I'm serious, I really am. But, yes, after the baby comes, I promise I'll take you to the fanciest restaurant in town and you can wear your slinky dress."

Hannah pointed one finger in the air. "Not until I lose whatever weight doesn't evaporate when Patty is born."

"How...how long will that take?"

She shrugged. "I don't know. I've had friends who fit into their old jeans the day they came home from the hospital. Others had to exercise and diet for weeks."

Weeks? Ted thought. How many weeks? He'd promised, fool that he was, to take her out to dinner. Promises made, were promises to be kept.

But, oh, hell, the agony of it all. Each day he was with Hannah and the baby, impersonating a family, sharing Patricia Elizabeth while knowing he had to leave them, was going to be torture.

Oh, Lord, what he wouldn't give for things to be different, for the truth *not* to be the truth. If only he was whole, the man that Hannah deserved to have. If only—

"Ted!"

"Huh?" he said, snapping back to attention.

"Daisy is crawling up the Christmas tree!"

"Oh, Lord. Hey, you," he said, hurrying across the room. "We have an angel on the top of that tree, thank you very much. The job has been filled."

And her heart had been filled, Hannah mused, with Ted. Forever.

* * *

A week later, Ted sat on the sofa in his living room, the telephone receiver propped between his head and shoulder.

"So, there you have it, Mom," he said. "Hannah is my pregnant neighbor, and we've been seeing a lot of each other. She made me promise to tell you about the baby before you met her so you wouldn't be caught off guard, not knowing what to say, or whatever."

"I see," Susan Sharpe said. "Yes, it's better that we know so it won't create an awkward moment. That poor girl. Imagine having such a heartless husband. She's well rid of him."

"No joke."

"But Hannah certainly has a lot to deal with. Tending to a new baby is difficult enough, even if you have help at first, but Hannah has no family."

"Well, the MacAllisters treat her as one of the clan. Hannah's teacher friends don't have any kids, but the MacAllisters make up for it. Deedee, Andrea, Jenny, Jillian, the whole gang will pitch in, I'm sure."

"And you, Ted?"

"Me? Oh, well, I can run errands for Hannah when I'm off duty. You know, go to the store for diapers and stuff like that. Besides, I had a long talk with Patricia Elizabeth about being a good baby, sleeping through the night early on, not hollering unless she has a real red-alert situation. Patty and I understand each other."

"You sound as though you're... Oh, what words shall I use?...attached, emotionally involved, with Hannah and her baby."

Ted grabbed the receiver and got to his feet, pacing as far the telephone cord would allow.

"Ted?"

"Well, sure, I'm emotionally involved, as you put it. Look how quickly *you* had an emotional reaction to Hannah's situation. Hey, the Sharpes are nice people, you know."

"Somehow, dear, I don't think my feelings are coming from the same place as yours are. Well, we won't get into that."

"Good idea," he said, frowning.

"I'm looking forward to meeting Hannah, and I want to knit something for the baby. I assume that Hannah had an ultrasound since you referred to the little one as Patricia Elizabeth. That's such a lovely name. I'll make her a pink sweater, cap and booties."

"No, Hannah didn't have that test."

Susan laughed. "Then Forrest MacAllister must have declared The Baby Bet to be officially in operation and predicted that Hannah will have a girl."

"No, he said she'd have a boy on New Year's Day. That's where he put his twenty bucks. *I* announced that Patty will be born on Christmas. Forrest is going to lose The Baby Bet for the first time."

"You're that positive, are you?"

"Yup."

"Very interesting. Yes, that is *very* interesting."

Ted stopped his trek back and forth in front of the sofa.

"It is?" he said. "Why is it so interesting?"

"It's just motherly wisdom rising to the fore, Theodore."

"I hate it when you call me Theodore. It usually means trouble for me one way or another."

"Tsk, tsk, that's your suspicious police-officer mind clicking into gear. So, what did you buy Hannah for Christmas?"

"I've been shopping three times for her gift, but I can't find anything that rings my chimes."

"For heaven's sake, Ted, there's only a week left before Christmas."

"Plenty of time, plenty of time. I got Patty a cute stuffed kitten that looks just like Daisy. Oh, Daisy is the kitten I bought for Hannah so her apartment would seem more like a home. It worked, too. Daisy is nuts. She's into climbing up the Christmas tree."

"You've never fussed with a tree before."

"It's not in my place. I bought the tree and decorations, and Hannah and I put it up in her living room. Looks great. I got Daisy a little ball with a plastic mouse inside for Christmas."

"Interesting."

"Would you quit saying that?"

"I'm sorry, dear."

"Hey, listen, Mom. Hannah thinks she's fat and unattractive. You know what I mean? When you meet her, could you say something cool like being a new mom becomes her, or you're sure she was a very pretty pregnant person, or whatever?

"I think she looks beautiful and I've told her that a dozen times, but maybe if a new voice said it... No, forget it. By the time you get here, it won't matter anymore. Okay, that covers that."

Susan laughed softly.

"What?" Ted said. "I heard that funny little chuckle thing of yours. Dad always says that when you laugh like that, he and I might as well give up, because you're in your 'I know more than you know' mode."

"Do tell."

"No, *you* tell. What's going on in your nonstop brain?"

"Oh, this and that. Well, we're producing a huge telephone bill for you to pay. We'll get all caught up when we're together. Have a wonderful Christmas, Ted, and the same wish is extended to Hannah. Your father and I will see you a day or two after the holiday."

"Okay. Merry Christmas to you and Dad. Bye for now."

"Goodbye, dear."

Ted replaced the receiver, then stared at it with narrowed eyes.

His mother was a mother, *but* she was also a woman, which meant he didn't stand a chance of understanding her. What had Mrs. Susan Sharpe meant with her weird "interesting" and her all-knowing laugh?

There was no way his mom could have figured out he was in love with Hannah. He'd handled the conversation with genius-level expertise. Hannah was his neighbor. He'd befriended her during a rough time in her life because he was a nice guy. End of story.

Interesting.

"Hell," he said, "I'm going shopping for Hannah's Christmas present."

And this time, damn it, he was going to find the perfect gift for his beautiful Ms. Doodle.

And he did.

Ted stopped so abruptly in the crowded antique store that three people bumped into him. He maneuvered his way to the counter and waited impatiently for a clerk to assist him. A matronly woman finally arrived.

"May I help you, sir?"

"There," he said, pointing at the glass case. "That's what I want."

"It's an excellent choice. Would you like it gift wrapped?"

"Yes, please. Make it really pretty. The gift, paper, bow, everything has to be absolutely perfect."

"All right," the woman said, smiling. "You must love her very much."

"Yes," he said quietly. "Yes, ma'am, I love her very, *very* much."

Chapter Thirteen

On Christmas Eve, Hannah shared a hymnal with Deedee as the congregation sang "Oh, Come All Ye Faithful." The entire pew was filled with MacAllisters, and the church was aglow with candles.

The junior members of the family were in the nursery in the lower level. A large crowd was attending the early-evening service, and the building rang with joyous voices.

Ted and Ryan were the only ones not present, as they were on duty until midnight.

The organist finished the song with a flourish, then everyone sat down, eager to hear the reciting of the traditional Christmas story.

Hannah eased herself onto the hard, wooden pew, stifling a moan as her aching back sent the message to her brain that a soft pillow would be a welcome addition.

"Are you all right?" Deedee whispered to Hannah.

Hannah nodded. "I'll live. I think."

"We can scoot out of here if you want," Deedee said quietly. "These pews aren't very comfortable under the best of circumstances, let alone your condition. Trust me, I understand. You ache from head to toe."

Hannah crossed her eyes to emphasize her total agreement with Deedee's evaluation, causing Deedee to smother a burst of laughter.

"Shh," Forrest said.

Deedee poked him in the ribs with her elbow.

Hannah directed her attention to the minister who was reading the Christmas story with a deep, rich voice that held everyone spellbound.

Just listen, she told herself. She would *not* dwell on her aching back, nor the fact that she had to go to the bathroom. She'd ignore the continual kicks and pokes as the baby did a gymnastics routine.

"Oh," she gasped as a pain shot across her stomach.

"Hannah?" Deedee said, her voice hushed.

Hannah shook her head and patted Deedee's leg to assure her that all was well.

Oh, please, Hannah silently begged the minister, talk faster. There was a very large, extremely pregnant and uncomfortable woman here who wanted to go home and sink onto her marshmallow sofa.

As another sharp pain radiated through her abdomen, Hannah shifted on the pew, settled, then wiggled again. She took a deep breath, exhaled and told herself to relax. Her eyes widened as the baby delivered a swift kick, then another.

"You're out of here, Hannah," Deedee whispered. She leaned toward Forrest. "Hannah is miserable sitting on these pews, and I'm taking her home. Pass the word."

Forrest nodded and turned to whisper in Jillian's ear. The message was sent along the pew, MacAllisters nodding in understanding one by one.

Deedee reached under the pew to retrieve their purses, then flapped her hands at Hannah. Attempting to rise, Hannah failed, then gripped the back of the pew in front of her and leveled herself to her feet.

In Deedee's car, Hannah sighed.

"Thank you, Deedee," she said. "I'm sorry you're missing the Christmas Eve service, but I appreciate this so much. I shouldn't have come, but I really wanted to, and—"

"Don't apologize," Deedee said. "You gave it your best shot." She maneuvered expertly through the surging traffic. "I'll stay with you until Ted gets off duty. When I don't show up back at the church, someone from the family will take Teddy home and wait for Ryan to get there."

"No, please don't even think of staying with me. I just want to get into a caftan and stretch out on the bed. I'll be fine, Deedee."

"Are you sure?"

"Yes, I'm positive. The pew was just too uncomfortable. I should have known better. Oh, my goodness, I'll be so glad when this baby is tucked in her crib, instead of in *me*."

Deedee laughed. "I know the feeling. The last few weeks are beauts. Since Forrest always wins The Baby Bet, you can at least count down the hours until New Year's Day."

"I said I didn't want to have a baby on Christmas, but the way I'm feeling now, I just might start hoping that Ted wins The Baby Bet."

"Ted certainly was adamant about Patricia Elizabeth being born on Christmas Day." Deedee stopped at a red light and looked over at Hannah. "Tell me to shut up if you want to, but I can't for the life of me understand why Ted hasn't asked you to marry him."

Join the club, Hannah thought dryly. It was a question that hammered at her peace of mind relentlessly. She was trying so hard to accept things as they were, but it was difficult, so very, *very* difficult.

"Ted obviously is in love with you," Deedee went on, accelerating as the light turned green. "Everyone in the family is aware of how he feels about you, and you love him in return. And the baby? Gracious, Ted Sharpe is ten times worse than Ryan was as far as fussing over you, hovering around like a frantic father-to-be."

"Ted has been wonderful," Hannah said quietly, "and, yes, I love him more than I can even begin to tell you."

"Then why, why, why aren't you two married?"

"That's not . . . not what Ted wants, I guess."

"You guess?" Deedee said. "Haven't you sat down and discussed it?"

Hannah shook her head. "There's no point in doing that. Ted knows how I feel about him. He loves me, too, Deedee, and he loves Patty. It's all in place, just as it should be."

"But?"

"But Ted obviously doesn't want any part of being a husband and father, a married man. The structure of our relationship as it now stands is apparently what he prefers for the future, as well."

"He's a dolt. I could wring his neck. Darn it, Hannah, I just don't understand him."

"I don't, either. All I can do is accept things the way they are."

"Well, drat. I swear, when men got their supply of muscles, they were shortchanged on brains."

Deedee saw Hannah safely into the apartment, hugged her while wishing her a Merry Christmas, and parted with the reminder that everyone was due at the senior MacAllisters at two o'clock the next afternoon for Christmas dinner and the exchanging of gifts.

Hannah took a quick shower, hoping the warm water would ease some of her aches and pains. It didn't. She put on her favorite faded blue terry-cloth robe and looped the sash loosely over her stomach.

With a weary sigh, she plugged in the Christmas tree, then fed Daisy. Deciding a mug of hot chocolate sounded appealing, she headed to the kitchen, only to stop halfway there as another hot pain radiated across her lower abdomen. Catching her breath, she continued on her way.

As she waited for the chocolate drink to warm in the microwave, she pressed her fists against her lower back.

"Oh, my back, my back," she said aloud, then looked at Daisy who was polishing off her dinner. "I have a roaring toothache in my back, Daisy."

The kitten looked at her with what Hannah labeled a bored expression, then began to wash her paws.

"Thanks for the sympathy," Hannah muttered, patting her stomach. "How are things in there, kiddo? It's nap time, so knock off the rock and roll. Please, Patty?"

A few minutes later, Hannah was settled in the straight chair which she'd turned to face the tree, taking small sips of the hot drink she'd poured into a festive ceramic Christmas mug.

"Oh-h-h," she moaned as another pain hit.

She rolled her eyes heavenward.

At this rate, she knew, she'd never be able to sleep, and she was thoroughly exhausted. She'd drag through Christmas Day in a fog, probably only half-aware of what was going on. Grim. Very grim.

She wasn't concerned about the pains she was having, as it had been explained in her childbirth classes that this sort of thing was very common in the last stages of pregnancy. Unless the pains were coming in steady intervals with increasing intensity, they were to be ignored.

"Easy for them to say," Hannah said, frowning. "Ignored? Oh, right." She paused. "Ow! There's another one. Ignored? Ha! No way. Hannah, shut up and quit feeling sorry for yourself.''

She wiggled further into the chair to give her aching back as much support as possible, and gazed at the pretty tree while she drank the hot chocolate.

Several hours later, Ted and Ryan got into the patrol car and closed the doors.

''You're a soft touch,'' Ted said, chuckling. ''The guy was speeding, MacAllister, and you let him off with a warning.''

''Yeah, well, I looked at my watch and saw that it was two minutes after midnight. I can't ticket a guy on Christmas, for Pete's sake.''

''Soft touch,'' Ted said decisively. ''Let's head on in. Our shift is over.''

''Yup,'' Ryan said, turning the key in the ignition.

He waited for an opening in the traffic, then eased onto the road. Cars traveling in both directions immediately reduced their speed at the sight of the patrol car.

''Well, hell,'' Ryan said, ''it's Christmas.''

Ted looked over at him. ''What's your problem, Mr. Scrooge? You like Christmas as much as a kid does.''

''Yeah, I know. It's a great day, very special, which is why I can't go through it with a guilty conscience. I have a confession to make.''

''Oh, yeah?''

''Yeah. Ted, remember when you told me you were going to leave Hannah because you can't have kids?''

"Of course I remember. What did you do? Break your word and tell Deedee that I'm sterile?"

"No, no, I haven't said a word to her about that conversation. She has no idea why you haven't asked Hannah to marry you. I think she's coming to the conclusion that you're certifiably insane."

"Then what's the big confession about?"

"I said I agreed with you, that you were absolutely right about leaving Hannah, and you should hit the road after the baby was born."

"MacAllister, I really don't feel like going over this territory again. Things are tough enough for me without—"

"I was lying through my teeth," Ryan interrupted. "Blowing smoke."

"What?"

"Oh, hell, I was trying reverse psychology on you. It's worked before. I've done it to you, you've done it to me. I was hoping you'd get really ticked at me for saying what I did, think about it, argue it in your mind and come to the conclusion that you were wrong and I was full of bull for agreeing with you."

"You're a great buddy," Ted said with a snort of disgust. "Thanks a lot."

"Damn it, Ted, you wouldn't listen to reason, and I knew it. I tried another approach, that's all. But now it's officially Christmas and I have to clear the air.

"Sharpe, you're a fool if you walk away from Hannah without giving her a chance to hear the truth and make her own decision regarding it."

"Look, MacAllister—"

"No, you look. Look at what you have with a sen
sational woman who loves you. How many times d
you think love like that comes into a person's life?
almost lost Deedee because I wouldn't listen, and wa
a stubborn jerk.

"Well, you're the jerk on this trip, Ted. You're go
ing to destroy something beautiful, rare, special. And
Hannah won't even understand why you did it. I
stinks, it really does. Damn it, you owe it to her to tel
her the truth. You have no right to make her deci
sions for her."

"Are you finished yet?" Ted said, narrowing hi
eyes. "You're really pushing me."

"Somebody has to. You can deck me when we ge
to the station if you want to, but all that will do is give
you a busted hand. You're running, Ted, like a cow
ard. *A coward.* It'll take guts to go to Hannah and tel
her the truth. You, apparently, are fresh out of cour
age."

Ted opened his mouth to deliver an angry retort,
then snapped it closed again in the next instant. He
drew a shuddering breath, then dragged both hands
down his face.

"You're right," he said, his voice gritty with emo
tion. "Oh, damn, you're right. I should have done it
weeks ago. Then I copped out by convincing myself it
would be best to wait until after the baby was born,
because Hannah has enough on her plate now. That
was pure selfishness, because I want to see, to hold
Patty so very much.

"But what you said about having a guilty con
science on Christmas really hits home. I don't want

Hannah to remember this holiday as the one she spent with Ted Sharpe while he was living a lie.

"I have to tell Hannah why I'm leaving her. I'll do it before we go to your folks for Christmas dinner. We may not show up there once I've told Hannah that I'm walking out of her life in a few weeks."

"Ted," Ryan said quietly, "you just may not be going anywhere in the next few weeks except to buy a marriage license. Women, bless their weird minds, have earned a reputation for coming through in the crunch."

Ted shook his head, then stared out the side window.

"You'll tell her?" Ryan said.

"Yeah."

"Good. Merry Christmas, buddy."

"Mmm."

Several minutes passed in total silence, then Ted suddenly stiffened.

"'Yankee Doodle,'" he said.

"What?"

"Have you ever had a song pop into your head and bug the hell out of you?"

"Sure."

"I'm hearing 'Yankee Doodle' over and over."

Ryan shrugged. "So sing 'Jingle Bells' or something, and block out 'Yankee Doodle.'"

"No, you don't understand. It's a message from Hannah."

"It's a what?"

"It's a signal from Hannah, I know it is. Step on it, Ryan. Hannah's in trouble. She needs me."

"You've got it," Ryan said, pressing harder on th
gas pedal. "'Yankee Doodle'?"

"'Yankee Doodle,'" Ted said, nodding. "Hit th
siren and take me to the apartment complex. I have t
get to my Hannah. Now. *Right now.*"

Chapter Fourteen

A sob of fear escaped Hannah's throat as she pulled a caftan over her head with trembling hands. The terry-cloth robe she'd been wearing was in a sodden heap on the bathroom floor.

Dear God, she thought frantically, her water had broken and the excruciating pains were coming in rolling waves, one after the next.

She needed help.

She needed Ted.

Ted, she mentally begged. Please. Hurry. Ted, hear me, hear "Yankee Doodle." It's our secret message, remember? "Yankee Doodle." "Yankee Doodle."

She looked at the clock, knowing Ted was off duty and should be on his way home. But there was always the chance that he'd been delayed out in the field. She couldn't wait any longer. She'd have to deal with this herself, alone. *Alone.*

Dial 911, she thought. Yes, that was what she must do. No, first she'd unlock the door for the paramedics while she could still get that far, *then* make the call. Okay, good plan. *Move, Hannah.*

With her arms hugging her stomach, she stumbled from the bedroom, down the hall, and into the living room. Halfway to the door, another pain sliced through her, causing her to grip the edge of a chair, then sink to her knees, tears of panic streaming down her face.

"Ted," she whispered. "Please . . ."

When Ryan slammed on the brakes in the parking lot of the apartment complex, Ted bolted from the patrol car.

"Do you want me to radio for an ambulance?" Ryan yelled after him.

Ted stopped. "No. It may not be that serious. You go on into the station. No sense in both of us getting into trouble."

"Are you sure?" Ryan asked.

"Yes! Go! And I'll talk to you later," Ted yelled as he rushed across the parking lot toward the stairs.

Ted barrelled from the stairway, raced to Hannah's apartment and pounded on the door.

"Hannah! It's Ted. Open up. Hannah? I'm here. I heard 'Yankee Doodle' and I'm here. Hannah!"

Ted, Hannah's mind whispered. Oh, thank God, he'd come. He'd heard her, heard "Yankee Doodle."

She had to get to the door and unlock it, so that Ted could help her.

"Ted," she yelled. "I'm coming. Wait for me. I need you, Ted. Wait...for...me."

Every muscle in Ted's body tensed as he heard Hannah's plea. He curled his hands into tight fists at his sides, ordering himself not to kick in the door.

Wait for me.

Ah, Hannah. He'd waited a lifetime to find her. He was going to tell her the truth about himself, lay it all on the line and pray. It was time, long overdue.

But now? Right now? Dear heaven, Hannah, open the door!

He heard the clink of the chain, then the snap of the lock and grabbed the doorknob.

"Move back out of the way," he shouted. "I'm coming in, Hannah."

He opened the door just enough to slide through the opening and slammed it closed behind him. In the next instant, Hannah moaned and once again began to sink to the floor.

"Oh, Lord," he said, his heart racing.

He scooped her into his arms and hurried down the hall to place her on the bed. Bracing his hands on the pillow on either side of her head, he leaned over her.

"Hannah? What's going on, sweetheart?"

"Oh, Ted," she said, a sob catching in her throat, "you heard me, you heard 'Yankee Doodle.'"

"You bet I did. Talk to me. What's wrong?"

"The baby...Patty...I can feel...my water broke and the pains...I have to push, Ted...I... *Oh-h-h,*" she moaned, clutching her stomach.

Think, Sharpe, he told himself as sweat trickled down his chest and back. He'd taken a course in delivering a baby at the academy, but that was a century ago.

He couldn't do this.

He couldn't!

What if he made a mistake?

What if something happened to Hannah or Patty because of him, because he did something wrong?

No!

"I'll call for the paramedics." He snatched up the telephone receiver on the nightstand and punched in 911.

"Oh, oh, oh," Hannah said, panting. She raised herself to rest on her elbows. "Oh, God, the baby's coming right now, Ted."

"Not yet!" he yelled.

He rattled off the information to the person who had answered the telephone, then slammed the receiver back into place just as the woman told him to stay on the line.

"Ted!"

"Yes. Okay. Yes. I'll . . . I'll wash my hands. Yes, I need to do that."

He ran into the bathroom, emerged moments later, then dashed to the linen closet in the hall. He returned to the bed and dumped a stack of towels on the other side of Hannah. She sank back onto the pillow with a whimper.

Ted framed her face in his hands. "Hannah, I love you. You're going to be fine. Patty is going to be fine. I swear it. Trust me."

"I do trust you," she whispered. "I love you so much, Ted." She paused, then her eyes widened. "Oh, dear heaven."

Ted straightened and eased Hannah's caftan up over her large stomach.

Stay cool, Sharpe, he ordered himself. Get a grip. This is the most important thing you've ever done in your life. This is Hannah. This is Patty. These two are your world, your reason for being.

From a source unknown, a sudden calmness came over him, accompanied by a sense of determination and confidence. He moved to the foot of the bed as Hannah once again raised onto her elbows, gasping.

Ted's heartbeat roared in his ears.

"I can see her head, Hannah," he said. "Bend your knees. That's right. You're doing great."

"Push," she said, panting. "Push."

"Okay, go for it. I'm here with you, Hannah. Patty is definitely ready to say Merry Christmas."

"Oh-h-h. Oh, God. No. No more. Stop it, Ted, make it stop. The pain is ... *No-o-o.*"

"Push, Hannah."

"Yes, yes, yes. Push, push ... Gran. Gran!"

Ted extended his large hands and ...

She was there.

Patricia Elizabeth was born.

Ted caught her tiny head in the palm of one hand, her little bottom in the other, then laid her on the bed. After swiping a finger through her mouth to clear it, he reached for a towel.

"Ted?" Hannah said. "Ted?"

He wiped Patty's face gently. She opened her eyes, raised her fists, pulled up her knees ... and wailed.

"Oh, my God," Ted said, his voice ringing with awe and wonder. "A miracle. She's a miracle. Oh, Patty, you're so beautiful, so perfect. You're my daughter. The only one I'll ever have. You're mine."

"Ted!"

He snapped his head up to look at Hannah, tears brimming in his eyes. Lifting Patty, he placed her on Hannah's stomach.

"Oh, my, look at her," Hannah said, laughing and crying at the same time. "And listen to her. Hello and Merry Christmas, Patricia Elizabeth. Welcome to the world. Oh, Ted, I..."

The sudden sound of someone knocking loudly at the door of the apartment broke the magical spell that had woven around the trio in the bedroom. Ted ran to the door and flung it open.

"Paramedics, Officer," a man said, acknowledging Ted's uniform. "You've got a baby on the way here?"

"In the bedroom," Ted said, stepping back.

"Uh-oh, by golly," the second man who entered said. "What I'm hearing says that we're arriving a tad late." He smiled at Ted. "Score one for the cops, huh? How'd you get the call?"

"I belong here," Ted said. "They're mine. Hannah and Patty are... I helped deliver Patricia Elizabeth." He grinned. "Yeah, son-of-a-gun, I did."

"Good for you, Daddy," the man said, hurrying after his partner. "Congratulations."

Daddy.

"Whew," Ted said aloud as tears once again filled his eyes. He looked heavenward. "Thank you." He nodded. "Thank you."

Daisy lifted her head from where she'd been sleeping beneath the Christmas tree, meowed, yawned, then went back to sleep.

"Not enough excitement for you, Daisy?" Ted said, smiling.

One of the paramedics came into the living room.

"Everything is fine," he said to Ted. "We've tied and cut the baby's cord, and checked her over. She's A-OK and mad as blue blazes for being disturbed. Your wife is fine, too. We've called for an ambulance to take them to the hospital. You can follow us over. Your little girl was sure in a hurry to get here, wasn't she?"

"Yeah, she was. She actually sort of delivered herself but, man, I'll never forget witnessing that event. It was really something. Awesome. Humbling. You know what I mean?"

"You bet I do."

"I knew Patty was going to be born on Christmas," Ted said. "I just . . . knew."

"Well, she got the message, all right. I'm going down and wait for the ambulance."

"Yo," Ted whispered a few minutes later as the ambulance driver stepped into the bedroom where Hannah and Patty slept quietly.

"Santa Claus bring a baby here?" the driver asked with a smile.

Ted grinned. "He sure did, and she's the most beautiful baby girl in the world. She's fantastic, unbelievable. She looks just like her mother."

"Hey," the man said, laughing, "you're not a cop, you're a proud new father."

"You've got that straight," Ted said. "Hustle up, you guys, my ladies are waiting."

When Ted reached the hospital, he was told by a nurse that both Hannah and Patty were being examined, and that then mother and daughter would be put to bed.

"Can't I see them for five seconds?" he said.

The nurse smiled. "Not tonight."

"But I only waved at Hannah when they put her and the baby into the ambulance."

"Go home, get some sleep and come back in the morning. You've had quite an experience. I—" The telephone at the nurses' station rang, and the woman answered it. "Maternity... Yes... Wonderful... I'll tell him." She replaced the receiver.

"Tell who him?" Ted said. "Me?"

"Your daughter weighs six pounds nine ounces, and is perfect. Your wife is fine, and is being tucked into bed for a very well-earned rest. Please stop at the admissions desk and give them the information they need for their forms, then off you go."

"But—"

"Shoo, Daddy, and Merry Christmas to you. This is certainly one you won't ever forget."

"No," Ted said quietly, "I certainly won't. Thank you and Merry Christmas. Good night."

By the time Ted returned to Hannah's apartment, the rush of adrenaline that had been coursing through him had ebbed and was replaced by total exhaustion.

He changed the sheets on the bed, gathered the towels and the soggy bathrobe, and set the bundle by he door to be washed and dried. After feeding Daisy, he checked the apartment once more to be certain everything was shipshape, then headed down the hall to his own place with the load of laundry.

Once in bed, he willed himself to shut down his mind and get at least a few hours' sleep. At a decent hour, he'd call the MacAllister clan to inform them of Patricia Elizabeth's arrival.

"Hey," he said aloud, "I won The Baby Bet. Eat your heart out, Forrest. You've finally been unchampioned, hotshot."

Ted took a deep breath, let it out slowly, then mentally ordered sleep to numb his senses. But echoing in his mind was an amalgam of voices, snatches of words spoken by various people who had taken part in the miraculous events of the night.

Good for you, Daddy. Congratulations... You're not a cop, you're a proud new father... Your daughter weighs... Your wife is fine... Your wife... Your daughter... Wife... Daughter... Wife...

"Oh, God," Ted said, dragging his hands down his face.

If only it was true. If only Hannah *was* his wife. If they were married, then Patty's birth certificate could read: Patricia Elizabeth Sharpe; Mother... Hannah Sharpe; Father... Theodore Sharpe. They would be a family, the three of them, together.

Maybe it could still happen that way. If the hospital would hold up the birth certificate long enough for Hannah and him to be married, then...

But first he had to talk to Hannah. He had to tell her the truth about his being unable to give her more babies. After his conversation with Ryan, he'd decided to tell her in the morning.

Well, he still would. He'd go to the hospital, sit down by Hannah's bed, take her hand and pour out his heart and soul.

"Hannah, please," he said, his voice gritty with emotion. "Please, my beautiful Ms. Doodle, please agree to marry me, be my wife, allow me to be Patty's father. Please, Hannah?"

With a weary sigh, Ted drifted off into a restless slumber, tossing and turning through the remaining hours of the night.

Early in the morning, Hannah stirred and opened her eyes. Her heart quickened as she realized she had no idea where she was. In the next instant, she smiled, placing her hands on her relatively flat stomach.

Patty. Patricia Elizabeth had been born, she thought. Let it not be said that her daughter was among the ordinary. No, not Patty. She'd been in such a rush to grant the world the honor of her presence, she'd arrived on the bed in the apartment. And on Christmas, no less.

Ted had been wonderful. He'd actually heard, somehow heard, her cry for help as she'd mentally sent him the "Yankee Doodle" signal. She's been so frightened, *so alone,* but then Ted had come with his quiet authority, calm demeanor and his strength.

And Patty was born.

Hannah sighed in contentment as she envisioned the beautiful baby and the magnificent man who were filling her heart to overflowing. Patty and Ted.

She frowned slightly as she came fully awake.

Something niggled at her, disturbing her blissful state of mind, hovering in a shadowy corner just beyond her comprehension.

What was it? What could possibly be wrong on this glorious Christmas Day?

Concentrating even harder, she narrowed her eyes, then slowly they came, the haunting words that Ted had spoken to Patty immediately after the baby was born.

Oh, Patty, you're so beautiful, so perfect. You're my daughter. The only one I'll ever have. You're mine.

"Dear heaven," Hannah whispered. She hadn't really comprehended at the time what Ted was saying.

You're my daughter. The only one I'll ever have. You're mine.

A chill swept through her and she shivered as she pulled the blanket up to her chin.

What had Ted meant? A part of her mind was insisting that she should be thrilled that Ted considered Patty his daughter, that he loved her that much.

But another part of her felt threatened somehow, very frightened. Why was Patty the only daughter Ted would ever have? And there was something so ominous about the words, *You're mine.*

Oh, stop it, Hannah, she admonished herself. She was overreacting. Ted's emotional outburst had occurred at a highly charged moment. The man has just taken part in delivering a baby, for heaven's sake.

But still...

No, she wouldn't think about it anymore. She'd tuck it away, then discuss it with Ted when he came to see her. Yes, that was exactly what she would do. Fine.

You're my daughter. The only one I'll ever have. You're mine.

Hannah pressed trembling fingertips to her lips and fought against threatening tears.

"Merry Christmas," a nurse said, bustling through the doorway.

"What? Oh, yes, Merry Christmas to you, too."

"You certainly received a special gift, didn't you? Your baby is just a doll, and such a good girl. Fill her tummy, and she's right back to sleep."

"When can I see her?" Hannah said.

"It's breakfast for you first, then a wash. By then, it will be time for the little ones to come visit their moms. You can count her fingers and toes, hold her, sing her a lullaby, whatever suits your fancy. It will be an hour of bonding between you and your daughter."

You're my daughter. You're mine.

"Yes," Hannah said. "*My* daughter. Patty is *my* daughter."

"Is something wrong, dear?"

"I hope not. Oh, God, I hope not."

"Pardon me?"

"Nothing," Hannah said, managing a small smile. "I'm just so eager to hold Patty. So much of last night is a blur, and I need to see her, touch her."

"Of course you do, and you will. That will perk you right up, and you'll realize what a marvelous Christmas Day this is."

"Yes," Hannah said quietly. "Marvelous."

Ted telephoned the hospital as soon as he awoke and was informed that he could visit Hannah at noon. He then called Ryan and related the amazing series of events of the previous night.

"Well, I'll be damned," Ryan said. "Hannah really *did* send you a message with that 'Yankee Doodle' bit. Is that weird?"

"No, it's communication in rare form, Mac-Allister." Ted paused. "Man, the whole thing was beyond belief, Ryan. Seeing Patty born was... Helping to deliver her was... Hannah was so brave and...man, oh, man."

Ryan chuckled. "You're very articulate this morning. Merry Christmas, Dad."

"Yeah."

"Ted, did you get a chance to tell Hannah that you... No, I suppose you didn't."

"No, but I'm going to the hospital at noon to see her and I'll tell her then. When I come to your folks later, I hope I'll be announcing that Hannah and I are getting married. Correct that. I hope and *pray* I'll be saying that."

"Right on, buddy."

"Listen, will you pass the word along to the family about the baby?"

"Sure thing, but don't you want to call Forrest yourself? The Baby Bet champion has been dethroned."

Ted laughed. "It's about time. I'll leave the pleasure of informing him of that fact to you."

"I'll enjoy every minute of it. Give Hannah a Christmas hug from us."

"I will. Thanks, Ryan."

"Good luck, Ted. I sure hope that... Well, go for it. Everything will work out great."

"It has to. God, Ryan, I don't know what I'll do if I lose Hannah and Patty, I really don't. Well, I'll see you later."

"Yeah. Bye."

Ted slowly replaced the receiver, then took a deep breath.

"I love you, Ms. Doodle," he whispered.

When Ted entered Hannah's room at the hospital, she was sitting up, flipping idly through a magazine.

"Merry Christmas, Hannah," he said quietly as he walked toward her.

"Merry Christmas, Ted," she said, meeting his gaze.

Neither smiled, nor hardly breathed, as Ted stopped next to the bed. He lifted one hand to gently cradle her cheek, then leaned over to claim her mouth with his.

The kiss was exquisite; tender, loving and filled with hope.

Ted reluctantly broke the kiss, then sat down in the chair next to the bed. Hannah placed the magazine on the side table, then clasped her hands in her lap.

"You look very festive," she said.

Ted glanced down at the bright red sweater he wore over dark slacks.

"My mom made this for me last Christmas. She's a whiz with a pair of knitting needles."

"It's, um, it's a very nice sweater."

Ted leaned back in the chair and stared up at the ceiling for a long moment before looking at Hannah again.

"I need to talk to you about something important, Hannah," he said. "I realize I'm tense right now, and

I know why. The thing is, I get the feeling that *you're* uptight, too, and *that* I don't understand. Patty's all right, isn't she?"

"Oh, yes, she's wonderful," Hannah said, smiling for the first time. "They brought her to me and I burst into tears when they placed her in my arms. She's so beautiful, so tiny and perfect. I'll never be able to thank you enough for being there for me, for helping bring Patty safely into the world."

"I'll never forget it. It was an incredible honor to—" Ted stopped speaking and shook his head. "I can't find the right words. It's too big, too... I guess there's no way to describe being a part of a miracle like that." He paused. "Hannah, what's bothering you? What's on your mind?"

Hannah sighed. "I wish I could forget it, Ted, put it out of my mind and just concentrate on my blessings. I wish I could declare this a daffodils-and-daisies day, as well as the most fantastic Christmas I've ever had."

"But?"

"But I can't. I have to ask you what you meant by what you said to Patty when she was born. I need to understand it."

Ted frowned, then splayed one hand across his chest. "What *I* said to Patty?" He shook his head. "I don't remember speaking to her. I talked directly to her?"

"Yes." She drew a shuddering breath. "You said, 'Oh, Patty, you're so beautiful, so perfect. You're my daughter. The only one I'll ever have. You're mine.' Why, Ted? Why did you say that?"

Dear Lord, no! Ted thought frantically. He'd said all that aloud? He didn't remember doing it, saying it. He'd come to the hospital to explain things calmly and carefully to Hannah, but now he was in the position of having to defend himself. Damn it.

"Ted?"

"Hannah, look, this isn't going the way I planned it, not even close. I should have told you weeks, months ago, but..." He leaned forward and took her hands in his, propping his elbows on the bed.

"There's something you should have told me, but didn't?" she said, the color draining from her face, followed by a stricken expression.

"Ah, Hannah, please don't look at me like that."

"Are you saying there's something I don't know that will make you *someone* I don't know?"

"I came here to tell you today. Listen to me. Please? I love you, Hannah. I love you, and I love Patty. You believe that, don't you?"

"Yes, I believe that. But why did you speak those words to Patty when she was born?"

Ted's grip on Hannah's hands tightened and his voice was raspy with emotion when he spoke again.

"Because... because I'm sterile. I had the mumps when I was a teenager and I can't father a child. Not ever."

Hannah's eyes widened and her mind raced in a matching tempo with her thundering heart. She pulled her hands free and shifted slightly on the bed in an attempt to put distance between herself and Ted.

"Oh, dear God," she said, hardly above a whisper. "You want Patty. You see her as a way to be a father. You called her your daughter, said she was yours."

"Yes, but—"

"You said you loved me, but you didn't ask me to marry you. I kept wondering why, and now I know. You're not interested in marriage, in *me,* in being a husband. You're focused on being a father. You want Patty, only Patty."

"Hannah, no, it's not like that at all."

She leaned her head back on the pillows and closed her eyes.

"No, no," she said, "not again, not again. I believed in you, fell in love with you. I'd vowed to never again trust my judgment about any man, but I was convinced that I'd finally made the right choice and..."

She lifted her head and looked at Ted, tears spilling onto her pale cheeks.

"I was wrong...again," she said, a sob catching in her throat. "You're not who I believed you to be. You don't want to marry me because you love me. You see me as a way to have a child, to be a father, to nurture, love, watch her grow up, be a part of her life. All you wanted from me is my daughter. *My* daughter."

Ted lunged to his feet. "No! I came here to tell you that I can't give you more children. I know I should have told you the truth sooner, but I was scared to death, Hannah, so afraid you'd send me away.

"I had made up my mind that I'd leave you after Patty was born, get out of your life, so you could find a man who was whole, a man who could give you more babies. But then—"

"But then?" she interrupted, her voice rising. "Then what, Ted? A better idea, a genius-level plan? You'd ask me to marry you? You'd be able to have a daughter, and for that you'd put up with the nuisance and commitment of a wife?''

"Damn it, no! I walked into this room hoping, praying, you'd accept me as I am, as not totally a man. We'd raise Patty together, love her, be a family. She'd be *our* daughter. We could adopt more kids, Hannah, if you'd be willing to. We could have it all, don't you see?''

"What I see," she said, sobbing openly, "is that I've been betrayed one more time, one *last* time. What I see is that you're scrambling, frantically searching for a way to keep Patty in your life. Your proposal of marriage is your last-ditch effort to accomplish that.''

She dashed the tears from her cheeks with trembling hands.

"No. No, I won't marry you. Not ever. Go away, Ted. Leave me alone. Don't come near me, or my daughter. Patty is mine. *Mine.* You can't have my baby. You can't.''

Hannah covered her face with her hands and wept, sobs wracking her body. Ted lifted one hand toward her, then dropped it back to his side. The pain consuming him took his breath away. It was excruciating in its intensity.

He'd lost. He'd lost Hannah, the only woman he had ever, or would ever, love. He'd lost Patty, the daughter of his heart. He was a beaten man, empty, cold and so alone.

Hannah, his mind screamed. *No. Please!*

But he didn't speak. There was nothing more to say.

With a shaking hand, he took a small box from the pocket of his slacks. It was wrapped in gold paper and topped by a tiny matching bow. He set it on the bed,

hen turned and walked from the room, the sound of
Hannah's heartbroken crying beating against him like
physical blows.

A few minutes later, Ted stood in front of the nursery window, gazing at a peacefully sleeping Patty,
gazing at a miracle.

A moment later, he could no longer see Patricia
Elizabeth, because his vision was blurred by tears.

An hour later, Hannah opened the pretty box Ted
had left on the bed. Her tears started anew as she saw
he exquisite gift nestled in the fluffy cotton.

On a gold chain, carved from the finest ivory, was
a small and incredibly delicate daffodil.

Chapter Fifteen

Two days later, Ted paced his living room as he told his mother what had taken place and that he loved Hannah. His father was stretched out asleep on the sofa, enjoying an afternoon nap.

Susan and Dean Sharpe had arrived at Ted's apartment an hour before. With the special wisdom that mothers possess, Susan had waited until Ted brought up the subject of Hannah, rather than ask about her.

After Dean had dozed off, weary from the drive, Ted began his dismal tale, keeping his voice low so as not to awaken his father.

Ted stopped his trek and shoved a restless hand through his hair.

"There you have it," he said. "Great, huh? I blew it, Mom, big time. Hannah believes that I've stayed

ith her all these months because of Patty. I've lost
Iannah and I've lost Patty, too. I have no one to
Iame but myself. I knew, damn it, I knew, how im-
ortant truth and honesty were to Hannah."

He planted his hands on his hips and stared up at
ie ceiling, attempting to gain control of his emo-
ons. Looking at his mother again, he shook his head.

"I'm such a jerk," he said. "Hannah was deter-
iined never to trust her judgment again in regard to
er choice of a man. She had a major flaw, she said,
f not being able to tell if a man was really who he
resented himself to be, who she believed him to be.
o what do I do? I withhold the truth from her and
onfirm her opinion of men as frauds."

"Ted..."

"I was a fool to get involved with Hannah. I should
ave run like hell the minute I realized I was in love
vith her. I can't have a woman like Hannah in my life.
've known that for a very long time. Hannah is not
iine to have."

"Why on earth not?" Susan said. "You're a won-
ierful man. You're thoughtful, caring—"

"Mom, come on," he interrupted. "Reality check,
okay? I'm not a *whole* man. I can't give Hannah more
hildren. Look, I've never told you this because it
vould have served no purpose, but..."

He drew a shuddering breath, then said, "I heard
ou and Dad talking all those years ago after the doc-
or called to report that I was sterile. Oh, yeah, I heard
Dad say, 'Do you realize what he has been robbed of,
vhat this means?' In my own father's eyes, I wasn't
otally a man, never would be. I never felt as close to

him after that, because I knew I fell short, didn't measure up.

"Why do you think I went the swinging-bachelor route? Because I knew, Mom, that I couldn't ask any woman to marry me. I couldn't ask her to sacrifice her natural maternal instincts to want to have babies.

"What I did to Hannah was selfish and cruel. There's no excuse for my deception, for hurting her so terribly. I knew I couldn't have her. Hell, I've known how things stood ever since I was sixteen years old and heard Dad say—"

"You hold it right there," Dean Sharpe said, suddenly sitting up and swinging his feet to the floor.

"Well, that's dandy," Ted said, rolling his eyes heavenward. "I suppose you've been listening to this whole conversation."

"Indeed I have," his father said. "I kept silent because I realized you needed to get some things off your chest, and I didn't want to interrupt."

"So you eavesdropped, instead," Ted said with a snort of disgust. "You're cool, Dad, really terrific."

"Theodore, there's no call to be rude to your father," Susan said.

"That's all right, Susan," Dean said, "because I'm about to be rude to him. Ted, you're a dope."

"Thank you very much." Ted slouched onto a chair and glared at his father.

"Ted, listen to me," Dean said, his voice gentling. "I remember saying those words after the doctor called. They're as clear in my mind as though it were yesterday. You heard me. And?"

"And what?" Ted said.

"What did you do?"

"I ran. I bolted out the door and ran until I dropped. Then I cried. Okay, Dad? Is this what you want me to spill my guts about? I sobbed like a little kid because I would never be able to father a child, and because...because I was no longer the son for you that I'd been."

"Oh, my darling boy," Susan whispered. "No."

"Then when you two told me what the doctor had reported," Ted went on, his voice gritty, "I blew it off, said it was no big deal."

Dean shook his head. "So we didn't discuss it further. Dear Lord, I should have pushed you to talk about it. Ted, how can I ask you to forgive me? I'd sell my soul to turn back the clock to that day."

"Why?" Ted said. "Facts are facts."

"No, your facts are wrong," Dean said. "You ran out the door before you heard all of what your mother and I said."

Ted lifted one shoulder in a shrug.

"Ted, damn it, listen to me," Dean said, nearly shouting.

Ted blinked in surprise at his father's outburst and straightened in his chair.

"Okay, I'm listening," he said. "Calm down, will you? You'll get your blood pressure in an uproar, or something."

Dean leaned forward, rested his elbows on his knees and clasped his hands tightly.

"Son," he said quietly, "you listened that day with the mind of a sixteen-year-old boy, and you didn't even hear all that was said. It breaks my heart to realize you chose a life-style for yourself at that moment that was like an albatross around your neck all these years.

"Ted, when I said, 'Do you realize what he's been robbed of?' I wasn't referring to your manhood, nor did I for one second view you as less than a total man. My first reaction was pain for your loss, for never being able to witness the wondrous miracle of watching your wife grow big with your child, then seeing that baby born."

Ted stiffened, every muscle in his body tensing. "But I thought—"

"I now know what you thought," Dean said, "and my heart aches because of it."

"Do you realize that powers beyond our understanding," Susan said, "have set things to rights? You *have* witnessed the woman you love grow with a child you've come to love as though it were your own. You even had more than most other men, Ted. You were blessed by being given the opportunity to help deliver that baby, bring her into the world."

Ted nodded slowly, his mind racing.

"What you didn't hear that day you ran from the house," his mother said, "was my telling your father that you had so much love in your heart, even then at sixteen, that when you were grown, any child that you adopted would be, to you, truly yours, your very own. I said you needed only to find the right woman as your life's partner."

"And I agreed with your mother completely," Dean said. "I admitted that my first reaction that you'd been cheated out of something was wrong. Ted, I swear to you, I have never felt you were less of a man because you can't father a child. Never."

Ted dragged both hands down his face, then shook is head. "I don't know what to say to you two, es-ecially you, Dad. All these years, I believed . . . I isjudged you, I . . . Saying I'm sorry doesn't cut it, ot even close."

"I'm the one who is sorry, Ted," Dean said. "I ould have sat you down and talked the whole thing rough, instead of accepting your laid-back attitude s being how you really felt."

"Well, what's done is done," Susan said. "The im-ortant thing now is the present and future."

"Absolutely," Dean said. "That means Hannah nd Patricia Elizabeth. Theodore, you'd better mend nces with those special ladies, because I'll be very ross if I'm deprived of my daughter and grand-aughter."

"Mercy yes," Susan said. "I want to see Patty in the utfit I knitted her. Well, actually, I knitted her two utfits. So, Ted? Don't you think it's time to quit oping and start putting together a plan to fix this isastrous muddle? I have a daughter to hug and a aby to spoil. You'd best get on the stick, young an."

An achy sensation gripped Ted's throat as he look t his parents.

"I love you guys," he said softly. "I hope you know ow very much I love you."

"And we love you, son," Dean said.

"Always, darling," Susan said.

Dean cleared his throat and blinked back tears. Now then, it seems to me that you've got a battle on our hands to convince Hannah that you love her as

much as you love the baby. You're a Sharpe, and w
don't give up. Not ever. Understood.''

Ted smiled. "Yes, sir, I read you loud and clear.
He frowned in the next instant. "Damned if I know
what I'm going to do, though.''

"Listen to your heart," Susan said. "Oh, and qu
swearing so much. That's not the type of language t
use around Patty. Well, I'm ready for a bite to eat
Let's go to a restaurant before you're due on duty.''

Ted nodded and got to his feet. "Listen to m
heart? I sure hope it has something brilliant to say.''

Four hours into the duty shift, Ryan had ha
enough of Ted's total silence.

"How was your Christmas, Ryan?" Ryan said
"Great, really fun, and Teddy loved it. I covered fo
you after you called me at my folks, Ted, said yo
were bushed from impersonating the stork.

"Hannah? She came home from the hospital to
day. Her friend Laurie picked up her and Patty, say
ing she should be allowed to do at least that since he
weeks of training to be Hannah's birth coach wen
down the tubes.

"Deedee took a hamper filled with food for a cou
ple of lunches and dinners to Hannah this evening
She came home chatting like a magpie about tha
adorable little girl. I have a feeling I'm going to hear
'Let's have another baby' pretty quick here.

"Deedee says Hannah is feeling fine, but is quie
and doesn't smile much. Deedee thinks there's trou
ble in romance-land, but has no clue as to what hap
pened. She did mention that Hannah is wearing a
knockout necklace that is a daffodil carved from ivory

"Oh, yes, and Forrest is mad as hell at you for win-
ing The Baby Bet. He's convinced you cheated, but
an't figure out how in the world you did it.

"Well, it was nice talking to you, Sharpe."

"You're so cute," Ted said, shooting a glare in
Ryan's direction. "It boggles my mind."

"Well, hell, man, it's been like driving around with
damn corpse."

"Don't swear like that around Patty. I don't want
er hearing that stuff."

"Pardon me all to heck, *Dad*. What I want to know
s, how are you going to fix this mess? How are you
oing to convince Hannah you love her and want to
pend your life with her *and* Patty? Huh? Answer me
hat, Mr. Chatter Cheeks."

"I'm thinking," Ted said, none too quietly. "Okay,
MacAllister? I'm thinking about it so damn much, I'm
wearing out my brain. Hell, I've screwed this up so
adly it's a sin."

"I can see it now. Patty's first and second words
poken will be *damn* and *hell*. Shame on you."

"Shut up."

Ryan chuckled. "Go back to silent thinking."

"Mmm."

Ted didn't speak for the remaining four hours of the
hift.

During the following days, while being careful not
o encounter Hannah in the hallway or elevator, Ted
ontinued to turn his thoughts inward; sifting, sort-
ng, going over a multitude of memories, recalling
details of times spent with Hannah, reliving events and
onversations.

The senior Sharpes informed him they were going to drive up the coast for several days. Ted absently told them to have a nice trip and he'd see them when they got back.

"Take care of yourself, dear," Susan said.

"Okay."

"Your sofa is on fire, dear."

"Okay."

Susan laughed. "Just keep thinking the way you are. You'll find your answers."

"Okay."

On New Year's Day, Ted slept until noon. He and Ryan had put in a hectic night shift dealing with holiday party goers, hauling half a dozen to jail to sleep off an overindulgence of alcohol. And now, having drawn duty on New Year's Eve, the pair had the next two days off.

Ted opened one eye, glanced at the clock and immediately decided he was hungry. As he started to get out of the bed, he stopped, sinking back onto the pillow.

"Wait a minute," he said aloud.

He didn't move, nor hardly breathe. Things finally began to fall into place, slowly, piece by piece, like a complicated puzzle coming together and making sense at long last.

"Yes!"

He flung back the blankets, then headed toward the shower.

A half hour later, Ted knocked on Hannah's door with the toe of his shoe, due to the fact that his hands were full.

* * *

Hannah tucked the blanket over a sleeping Patty, then hurried from the baby's room to answer the summons at the door. She peered through the peephole, but frowned in confusion as she realized she had no idea what she was seeing. Leaving the chain in place, she cautiously opened the door.

"Hello, Hannah," Ted said quietly. "May I come in? Please?"

"I... Yes." She closed the door, undid the chain, then reopened the door so Ted could enter. She looked at what he was holding. "That's the dollhouse you made."

Ted nodded, then crossed the room to set it on the coffee table. He took a box from the first floor of the dollhouse and set it next to it.

"This is the furniture." He straightened and turned to look at Hannah. "I'd like Patty to have this, if it's all right with you."

Ah, Hannah, he thought. His beautiful Ms. Doo-le was exquisite. She looked sensational in jeans and pretty yellow blouse, a daffodil-colored blouse. The necklace he'd given her was around her neck, falling to just above her breasts.

He wanted to take her into his arms, hold and kiss her, ask her to marry him and stay by his side for all time.

Oh, man, how he loved her.

"That's a lovely gift you're giving to Patty," Hannah said. "Thank you. I'm sure she'll treasure it when she's old enough to appreciate it."

Ted, Hannah's mind hummed. He looked so tired, just totally worn-out. She'd missed him so much,

ached for his touch and kiss, and the feel of his stron
arms encircling her in the wondrous and safe cocoo
of his embrace.

Oh, she loved Ted Sharpe with all that she was as
woman.

No, that wasn't quite right. She loved the Te
Sharpe she'd *believed* him to be, not the Ted he actu
ally was, not the Ted who wanted only Patty in his life

"I see you're wearing the necklace," Ted said.

The fingertips of one of Hannah's hands flutterer
to the delicate daffodil, then stilled, clutching th
flower.

"It's so pretty," she said. "Thank you for giving
to me."

"Sure." He paused. "Hannah, I'd like to talk
you. Please? Would you sit down?"

"Well, I..." She sighed. "Yes, all right."

She sat in a straight-backed chair, clasped her hand
tightly in her lap and stared up at him.

This is it, Sharpe, Ted told himself. The next fe
minutes were going to determine his entire futur
happiness. *Don't blow it.*

"Hannah," he said, too wired to sit down, "I'v
been doing a lot of thinking lately. In fact, all I'v
done is think. That day in the hospital, I felt I'd lo
you forever, that it was over, everything that ma
tered to me was gone, beyond my reach."

Hannah lifted her chin. "You mean Patty."

"No, damn it...excuse me. I'm not going to swea
anymore because Patty's first words are *not* going
be *damn* and *hell.*"

He drew a deep, shuddering breath, then let it ou
slowly.

"Okay. Will you listen, really listen to me?"

"All right, Ted."

"Months ago, you said you can't tell the good guys om the bad, and you shouldn't trust your own dgment about men."

"Yes."

"Well, *I* have a major flaw, too. I'm a coward. hen things get tough, I run. I finally figured that out ter nearly thinking myself to death the last few ıys."

"A coward? Ted, you're a police officer, a very od one. You can't possibly be a coward."

"Yeah, I'm a good cop. That's not what I'm refer- ng to. I'm talking about my personal life. Hannah, hen I was sixteen, I heard my dad telling my mom I as sterile from my having had the mumps. What did do? I ran. I bolted out the door before I heard ev- ything my parents had to say about the situation. I as a coward. I couldn't face what had happened, so an.

"That cowardice cost me the close relationship I'd d with my father. I was convinced he felt I was no nger a total man, a whole man, and I was no longer hat he wanted in a son."

He shook his head.

"It wasn't true. He didn't feel that way at all, and I ould have known that if I'd had the courage to stand rm, talk it through with him.

"Hannah, I did the same thing that day in the hos- tal. You told me how you felt, and it hurt me so very uch that I ran. I was such a coward, I couldn't han- e the thought of hearing more of your accusations.

The price tag this time? Your love, our future happ
ness, everything that is important to me."

He hunkered down in front of her and took h
hands in his.

"Hannah, I've stopped running. I'm gathering n
courage, stripping my soul bare, rendering myself t
tally vulnerable. Risky? Oh, yeah, it's risky, but you'
worth it.

"Hannah Johnson, my beautiful Ms. Doodle, I lo
you more than life. I want to marry you and spend tl
rest of my life with you as your husband. I also wa
to be Patty's father. Ah, Hannah, can't we be a far
ily, together? Have it all? That's what is in my hear
I swear it. I love you, Hannah. Oh, God, how I lo
you.

"If you can't marry me, be my wife, because I'
not capable of giving you more babies, then I'll ha
to deal with that...somehow. At least I'll know
wasn't a coward, not this time. I'm just a man, pu
and simple, who loves you will all my heart. Tota
whole and forever love, Hannah, that is what I ha
to offer you, from a total, whole and forever man.

"I can't give you more children, but I'm offeri
you myself, all that I am. It's up to you if that
enough. It's up to you."

Hannah flung her arms around Ted's neck wi
such force that he toppled backward, taking her wi
him. They ended up on the floor, Hannah stretche
out on top of him.

"Yes, I'll marry you," she said, her eyes filling wi
tears. "I listened, Ted, to what you said, and I *hea*
you. I realize how difficult it was for you to run tl

asks you just did. I feel so loved, so cherished, so special.

"On behalf of myself and my daughter, *our daughter,* I accept your proposal of marriage. I'd be honored to be your wife. Patty will be a fortunate child to have you for a father. Oh, my darling Ted, I love you so much, so very, very much."

Ted's tears mirrored those in Hannah's eyes, as he weaved his fingers through her silky hair and brought her lips to his to seal their commitment to forever.

Daisy strolled into the room, took one look at the nonsense taking place on the floor, and went in search of something to eat.

Epilogue

At the wedding of Hannah Johnson and Ted Sharpe, the bride carried a lovely bouquet of daffodils and daisies.

Patricia Elizabeth wore a yellow dress that had been knit by Susan Sharpe. During the ceremony, the baby was held in the arms of her loving grandfather, Dean.

At the reception, which was held at the senior MacAllisters' home, Jenny and Michael MacAllister announced they were expecting their second child.

"So, Forrest," Michael said, "are you going to be in charge of The Baby Bet when Jenny is due?"

"Not me," Forrest said, laughing and raising both hands. "I know when I'm licked. The new champion of The Baby Bet is Ted."

"Wrong," Ted said, encircling Hannah's shoulders with one arm, "the new champion of The Baby Bet are Mr. *and* Mrs. Theordore Sharpe. Take a look at the wedding presents Hannah gave me. I set them up by the cake."

The group moved closer and everyone smiled.

Lined up in a row were tiny wooden figurines for the dollhouse. The miniatures included a man, woman and four children. The children were each of a different nationality from around the world.

"Perfect," Deedee said.

"Yup," Ryan said.

"Babies, babies, babies," Deedee said with a wistful sigh. "Ryan, don't you think it's time we..."

"Yup," he said, then kissed her on the nose. "If Ted intends to continue to be The Baby Bet champion, we'll make him really work to retain the title."

"No problem," Ted said. "I can handle it, right along with the other titles I have."

"Husband and father," Hannah said, smiling at him with love shining in her eyes.

"Forever, Mrs. Doodle," he said, matching her smile. "Forever."

SPECIAL EDITION

COMING NEXT MONTH

#1027 PART-TIME WIFE—Susan Mallery
That Special Woman!/Hometown Heartbreakers
When Jill Bradford took the position of nanny to three adorable b[c]
she was determined that it stay a business arrangement. But the b[c]
father, Craig Haynes, wanted more than just a part-time mother or
He wanted Jill forever.

#1028 EXPECTANT FATHER—Leanne Banks
Caleb Masters was intelligent, gorgeous—everything
Glory Danson desired in a man. Becoming pregnant with his child
married for the sake of the baby…but would the expectant father a
mom-to-be find love ever after?

#1029 ON MOTHER'S DAY—Andrea Edwards
Great Expectations
When Alex Rinehart reunited Fiona Scott with the daughter she'd g[i]
up for adoption, he helped her save the child she thought she'd neve
again. And now that Alex and Fiona had found each other, Fiona ha
more than one reason to celebrate on Mother's Day.

#1030 NEW BRIDE IN TOWN—Amy Frazier
Sweet Hope Weddings
Belle Sherman had arrived and the town of Sweet Hope—and its r
eligible bachelor, Boone O'Malley—would never be the same aga
When these opposites attracted, there was no stopping Belle from [
the next bride in town, unless her groom got cold feet!

#1031 RAINSINGER—Ruth Wind
Daniel Lynch was a drop-dead handsome Navajo with black eyes a
an attitude to match. And suddenly Winona Snow found herself sh
her house with him! Soon this stubborn man held the key to her
future…and her heart.

#1032 MARRY ME, NOW!—Allison Hayes
She had to save the ranch, but first Dacy Fallon needed to convince
flame Nick Reynolds to accept her help. He wouldn't admit that the
attraction was as strong as ever, but Dacy was determined to win he
a cowboy groom.…

MILLION DOLLAR SWEEPSTAKES
AND EXTRA BONUS PRIZE DRAWING

As seen on TV!
Free Gift Offer

With a Free Gift proof-of-purchase from any Silhouette® boo
you can receive a beautiful cubic zirconia pendant.

This gorgeous marquise-shaped stone is a genuine cubic
zirconia—accented by an 18" gold tone necklace.
(Approximate retail value $19.95)

Send for yours today...
compliments of ▼ *Silhouette*®
™

To receive your free gift, a cubic zirconia pendant, send us one original proof
purchase, photocopies not accepted, from the back of any Silhouette Roman
Silhouette Desire®, Silhouette Special Edition®, Silhouette Intimate Mome
or Silhouette Shadows™ title available in February, March or April at your favo
retail outlet, together with the Free Gift Certificate, plus a check or money order
$1.75 U.S./$2.25 CAN. (do not send cash) to cover postage and handling, pay
to Silhouette Free Gift Offer. We will send you the specified gift. Allow 6 to 8 weeks
delivery. Offer good until April 30, 1996 or while quantities last. Offer valid in the U.S.
Canada only.

Free Gift Certificate

Name: _____

Address: _____

City: _____ State/Province: _____ Zip/Postal Code: __

Mail this certificate, one proof-of-purchase and a check or money order for pos
and handling to: SILHOUETTE FREE GIFT OFFER 1996. In the U.S.: 3010 Wa
Avenue, P.O. Box 9057, Buffalo NY 14269-9057. In Canada: P.O. Box 622, Fort I

FREE GIFT OFFER   079-KBZ-R
ONE PROOF-OF-PURCHASE
To collect your fabulous FREE GIFT, a cubic zirconia pendant, you must include this
original proof-of-purchase for each gift with the properly completed Free Gift Certifica

---

079-K

Available in April from
Silhouette's sassy new series

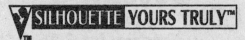
SILHOUETTE YOURS TRULY™

Every Groom's Guide To...
by Cait London

When Jillian Horton had to tell a husband-to-be that
his fiancée had jilted him a day before the wedding,
she soon found herself saying "I do" to wife-wanter
Cord Dougald. But her gorgeous new groom needed
a few lessons in Marriage 101....

Seducing Sydney
by Kathy Marks

Sydney Stone was just your average suburban
woman—until she received a mysterious love note
from an anonymous man. Suddenly, plain-Jane Sydney
had been transformed into a temporary glamour-puss
and was on the adventure of a lifetime!

Love—when you least expect it!

You're About to Become a

Privileged Woman

Reap the rewards of fabulous free gifts and benefits with proofs-of-purchase from Silhouette and Harlequin books

Pages & Privileges™

It's our way of thanking you for buying our books at your favorite retail stores.

**Harlequin and Silhouette—
the most privileged readers in the world!**

For more information about Harlequin and Silhouette's PAGES & PRIVILEGES program call the Pages & Privileges Benefits Desk: 1-503-794-2499

Silhouette®

SSE-f